D0875120

Griffin says he's leaving me.

I slipped my arms around Griffin, loving his smell and the angles of his shoulder blades and the way my head fit under his chin. I raised my face to his and we kissed softly.

"I don't want you to go," I whispered.

"I don't want to go," he said.

I knew he meant it. But you know what? That didn't make me feel better. In a way, it made me feel worse.

It wasn't the way I'd planned it. Not at all. When you're in love, things are supposed to work out. You know, because you've finally found the right person. Things are supposed to fall into place.

Right?

Party of Five™ books

Available from ARCHWAY Paperbacks

For orders other than by individual consumers, Pocket Books grants a discount on the purchase of **10 or more** copies of single titles for special markets or premium use. For further details, please write to the Vice-President of Special Markets, Pocket Books, 1633 Broadway, New York, NY 10019-6785, 8th Floor.

For information on how individual consumers can place orders, please write to Mail Order Department, Simon & Schuster Inc., 200 Old Tappan Road, Old Tappan, NJ 07675.

3 1705 00293 3957

party of five™

Julia: everything changes

ROSALIND NOONAN

BASED ON THE TELEVISION SERIES CREATED BY
CHRISTOPHER KEYSER & AMY LIPPMAN

WITHDRAWN

STATE LIBRARY OF OHIO
SEO REGIONAL LIBRARY
CALDWELL, OHIO 43724

AN ARCHWAY PAPERBACK
Published by POCKET BOOKS
New York London Toronto Sydney Tokyo Singapore

The sale of this book without its cover is unauthorized. If you purchased this book without a cover, you should be aware that it was reported to the publisher as "unsold and destroyed." Neither the author nor the publisher has received payment for the sale of this "stripped book."

This book is a work of fiction. Names, characters, places and incidents are products of the author's imagination or are used fictitiously. Any resemblance to actual events or locales or persons, living or dead, is entirely coincidental.

AN ARCHWAY PAPERBACK *Original*

An Archway Paperback published by
POCKET BOOKS, a division of Simon & Schuster Inc.
1230 Avenue of the Americas, New York, NY 10020

A PARACHUTE PRESS BOOK

Copyright © 1997 by Columbia Pictures Television, Inc. All Rights Reserved.

Columbia Pictures Television is a SONY PICTURES ENTERTAINMENT Company.

All rights reserved, including the right to reproduce this book or portions thereof in any form whatsoever. For information address Pocket Books, 1230 Avenue of the Americas, New York, NY 10020

ISBN: 0-671-01721-7

First Archway Paperback printing November 1997

10 9 8 7 6 5 4 3 2 1

PARTY OF FIVE and its characters are trademarks of Columbia Pictures Television, Inc.

AN ARCHWAY PAPERBACK and colophon are registered trademarks of Simon & Schuster Inc.

Cover photo courtesy of Columbia Pictures Television, Inc.

Printed in the U.S.A.

Julia: everything changes

Prologue

Fall

I closed the door of my house and glanced down the steps.

There he was. Shaggy brown hair, hazel eyes, ripped jeans covering his long legs. I said his name softly, to myself.

"Griffin."

My heart was doing its little drum solo, the way it did whenever I saw him. So what if we'd been together for a couple of months now? I still got that feeling every single time.

I know, seriously corny. But there was this . . . *thing* that went on between us. An extra level of communication. Like he was sending me messages between the words.

Not that everything was perfect between us. Lately it seemed that Griffin was just kind of drifting through life without a plan—which bothered me. But still . . . just watching him lean over the car, tightening the bolts on the mirror, I got this incredible warmth inside.

He hadn't spotted me yet. I bounded down the stairs.

"Hey," I called, jumping from the bottom step to the sidewalk. A chilly wind blew my hair into my eyes. "What's up? How's the job hunt going?"

He didn't look up at me. "I've kind of got that covered."

My stomach tightened abruptly. Remember what I said about reading between the words? Something was up. I could feel it.

"Oh," I said flatly. It wasn't a question. But he answered anyway.

"Yeah, um—this buddy of mine made some calls and . . . I'm going to catch up with the boat down in San Diego."

"The boat?" For a second I couldn't even make sense of the words. What boat?

"They're loading up for Australia," he went on. "The money's decent. And there's plenty of time to think."

Boat . . . Australia . . . Was he talking about the merchant marine ship? The one he just quit working on at the end of the summer?

I began to feel a coldness in my chest. "You mean . . . you're leaving? Again?"

At last Griffin stopped fixing the car mirror. His eyes were serious and kind of sad. "I've been thinking about what you said, Julia. About me needing things in my life that matter. Besides you."

"But—I never said anything about *leaving*," I told

him. My throat felt tight. The way he'd sprung this on me . . . "I thought we were going to figure this out together. And now you're just . . . running away."

Griffin held his hands up, as if I was moving too fast. "I'm coming back," he said. He put down the tools and faced me. "That's the whole point. I just— everything's messed up with us now, you know? And that's kind of my fault. I mean, you're starting to hate me—"

"I don't hate you," I protested.

"You know what I mean. I don't want to screw this up. And if I keep hanging around here, I'm going to make things worse." He put his hands on my shoulders and looked me in the eyes. "I'll be back," he said softly. "I just have to figure out a few things. About me. About what's important to me."

I shook my head, trying to blink back the tears that stung my eyes. "I don't get it, Griffin. I really don't." I swallowed hard. "I mean, if we really love each other, the whole point is that we're supposed to be together. We're supposed to be here for each other. And the stuff about figuring out what's important? It's not something for you to run off and do alone."

He slumped back against the door of the car. "I'm sorry. I mean, I want to be with you. You're this incredible thing in my life. But the ship? This job? It's the only right thing I can do. You keep telling me that I need something in my life. Like a job or ambition or something. I've got to find that."

"I was hoping you'd find it here, with me," I said.

His eyes were full of pain. "I just—can't." He pulled me into his arms, running his hands over my hair, my shoulders, my arms. His touch was rough, sort of desperate.

"It's the only way, Jule," he whispered in my ear.

I pushed him away. "So where does that leave me?" I demanded. My voice was ragged with tears. "Do you want me to promise to wait for you or something? Because I don't think I can do that. Not when I don't know where you are or when you're coming back or anything."

A warm tear slid down my cheek. I couldn't hold it back. I reached up to wipe it away, but Griffin was faster. He pressed his palm gently against my face.

"All I know is that I'll be back," he said softly. "I'm not leaving because of you. I'm going because of *me.*"

I picked at the zipper on his leather jacket. "Is that supposed to make me feel better?"

"Hey, you're the one who keeps telling me that we have to get out there and go for it," he pointed out. *"You're* the one with the twenty-year plan. Stanford University. Then a world tour. Then a couple of books about the world tour."

"Yeah, but . . ." I trailed off. It was kind of true. Okay, maybe I didn't have the next twenty years totally mapped out, but I had definite plans for my life. I wanted Griffin to have a plan for *his* life, too.

Just not this plan. Not a plan that involved leaving me.

"Then, like, two point five kids and a house in the suburbs," Griffin added.

"I will *never* have a house in the suburbs," I protested, but through my tears I almost laughed. Griffin knew me so well!

I slipped my arms around him, loving his smell and the angles of his shoulder blades and the way my head fit under his chin. I raised my face to his and we kissed softly.

"I don't want you to go," I whispered.

"I don't want to go," he said.

I knew he meant it. But you know what? That didn't make me feel better. In a way, it made me feel worse.

It wasn't the way I'd planned it. Not at all. When you're in love, things are supposed to work out. You know, because you've finally found the right person. Things are supposed to fall into place.

Right?

Chapter 1

January

I wish I could go with you," my sister Claudia said. She climbed onto a stool at the kitchen counter and poured milk on her cornflakes. "I've always wanted to see Stanford. You know, since Mom went there." She tucked her shiny dark hair behind her ears and turned to the task at hand—breakfast.

I shrugged. "So come."

"Can't." She shook her head. "Violin lesson." Claudia is a really talented violin player. And dedicated, too. Which is pretty cool for a thirteen-year-old kid.

I poured cereal into a bowl and reached for the milk carton. Empty. "We're out of milk again?" I grumbled, wheeling around toward my oldest brother, Charlie. He was supposed to be in charge of stocking groceries this week.

He put his hand over the phone, annoyance in his

brown eyes. "Look in the fridge." Raking his hair off his forehead, he went back to the call. "Yeah, and we need Vidalia onions. What are they running these days? Whoa, that's way too much. Can't you cut me a break?"

He was talking to a restaurant supplier, ordering stuff for Salinger's, the restaurant that our parents started. Charlie manages it now that our parents are gone. They died a few years ago in a car crash. And since Charlie is the oldest Salinger kid, he manages our family, too.

Well, he tries.

"Ouch!" Charlie yelped as a can of crushed tomatoes whacked him in the ankle. He bent down, clutching the phone in one hand and rubbing his ankle with the other. He glared at my three-year-old brother, Owen, who was building a fort out of canned goods. "Would you cut that out, Owe?"

"My fort fall down," Owen moaned.

"Careful, Owen," Claudia warned. "Those cans are heavy."

"Heavy!" He grinned, rolling a can of beans across the floor as if he were bowling.

With his curly, light brown hair and the dimples in his cheeks, Owen reminds me a lot of my other brother Bailey. Right down to his ability to get into all kinds of trouble.

I stepped over a stack of tuna cans on my way to the refrigerator and pulled out another carton of milk.

"Now, what about Portabello mushrooms?" Charlie said into the phone. "I'm going to need six pounds. Right. Thanks."

"No, Owen!" Claudia shrieked as Owen began rolling cans at her violin case.

Just another morning in the Salinger house.

Believe it or not, today wasn't as hectic as usual. It was Saturday, so Claudia and I weren't rushing off to school. I was waiting for Bailey to pick me up. When Bailey started college last fall, he moved into his own apartment. For the rest of us, home is an old Victorian house at the top of a typical San Francisco hill.

Anyway, Bailey and I were heading over to Palo Alto to check out Stanford University, my first-choice college.

It was January of my senior year of high school, and everybody I knew was going nuts trying to pull together college applications. Including me. I'd applied for early decision from Stanford, so the letter should be coming any day now. My friend Libby had applied early decision to Harvard, and she got her acceptance letter just last week. Man, was she lucky!

Which reminded me. I owed her a phone call. She'd left me a message a couple of days ago. I should call her back right away, I thought. Maybe her luck would rub off on me.

The phone rang again. Charlie leaped to answer it. "Charlie Salinger," he said in his dynamic-businessman voice.

A second later his face darkened. "Just a second," he growled, and held the phone out to me. "It's Sam."

I gave him a look as I took the phone. From the expression on his face, you'd think I was dating a serial killer.

"He's way too old for you, Jule," Charlie muttered for the zillionth time.

I covered the mouthpiece with my hand. "He's twenty-four. Younger than you," I reminded Charlie. "You make it sound like I'm dating a senior citizen."

Yes, it's true, I was seeing someone else. I mean, Griffin had been gone for over two months already, and I had no idea when—if—he was coming back. I couldn't just sit around waiting for him forever. And Sam was so nice . . . and so gorgeous!

I turned my back on Charlie. "Hey. What's up?" I said into the phone.

"You," Sam answered. "Me. Coffee House. This afternoon."

Smiling, I poured milk onto my cereal. "I'm there," I said. "So—what's new?"

"Jule." Charlie folded his arms. "I'm waiting for a call."

I made a face. "Look, I can't talk right now," I told Sam. "See you this afternoon, okay?"

"Thank you," Charlie said as I hung up.

A second later the phone rang again. "Charlie Salinger," Charlie said.

"Has anyone seen my rosin?" Claudia asked, fishing through the kitchen drawer. "It always disappears the day of my lesson."

"Nope." I leaned over the cereal bowl for a big bite.

"I wonder if it's the same," Claudia mused.

"Your violin rosin?" I mumbled through a mouthful of flakes.

"What?" Claudia blinked. "Oh, no, I mean Stanford. I wonder if it's the way it was when Mom went there. Do you know the name of the dorm she lived in?"

I shook my head and swallowed as I heard the kitchen door open behind me.

Bailey stepped in, his hair still a little wet from a shower. "Ready to go?" he asked, his face lit with one of those dimpled smiles that makes girls go all soft for him.

Yeah, Bailey's got the look—a square jaw and deep blue eyes—he's the only Salinger who doesn't have your basic brown eyes—and a hard, solid body that makes him a pretty good wrestler.

He picked up Owen and tossed him in the air till Owen shrieked. "Gotcha! Gotcha! Gotcha!" Bailey teased.

"Hey!" Charlie waved at them to pipe down. "I'm trying to do some business here."

Rolling his eyes, Bailey swung Owen to the floor. "If we leave now, we'll miss the big Saturday rush," he told me.

"No, we're already too late. It's going to take us forty-five minutes no matter what. So give me a minute to finish eating," I said.

"Breakfast?" Bailey reached for a box of cereal. "Don't mind if I do."

"Do you have any idea how lucky you are?" Bailey asked me. We were hiking down one of the paths at Stanford—and I mean *hiking*. The campus is huge. There are tall palm trees and grassy hills and buildings with red-tiled roofs. "I mean, to go here? You are totally lucky. Jackpot."

"Luck doesn't have a lot to do with it, Bay," I said. "More like studying for tests. Getting good grades. Is this ringing any bells?"

"Sorry. I'm a little deaf," Bailey said. He grinned at a passing female student. "You're going to like it here, Jule."

"*If* I get in," I said, crossing my fingers.

"Give me a break." Bailey frowned, adjusting his sunglasses. "You'll get in. You've only been planning for it since the day you were born."

"True. But if I'm such a great student, where is my stupid acceptance letter?"

Bailey shrugged. "Let's march right over to the dean of admissions and remind him just who he's messing with."

I laughed. "Yeah, right."

Don't let the sarcasm fool you. Bailey is sort of the heart of our family. He thinks I'm really smart, and sometimes he admits it (almost). He's probably Claudia's best friend. Owen adores him. And Bailey can even get Charlie to change his mind sometimes— which is just about impossible for anyone else.

I guess every family needs someone like Bailey. You know, someone to keep you all flying straight and level. A fixer.

A Frisbee landed at our feet. I picked it up and flung it back to one of the guys playing on the lawn. Ahead of us was a student café, where tables spilled out onto the patio. Most of the furniture was stacked up, but a few students had pulled down chairs to sit and soak up the sun, which felt warm for January.

Bailey glanced at the map in his hand, then pointed ahead. "That must be Grenada Hall. And the library's over there. And did you see that swimming pool, Jule? Incredible. This place is like a hotel. Four years in a hotel."

"Yup." I grinned. I felt charged up by the energy that seemed to hover over the campus.

"Are you getting psyched?" Bailey asked, squeezing my arm. "You don't look psyched enough to me."

"I'm psyched already, okay?" I said, shaking him off. "Who appointed you to the cheerleading squad?"

"I don't know. There's just something special, knowing that Mom went here. Okay, call me sentimental. But it's really cool that you're following in her footsteps."

I rolled my eyes. "You're sentimental," I said. "And I hate that stuff about following Mom. I mean, it's my decision. My life. I'm still doing things my way."

"Whatever." Bailey shoved the map into the pocket of his baseball jacket. "I'm starved. Let's head over to . . ." His voice trailed off as he stared at a passing student. "Hey. Kate? Kate Fordham, right?"

The girl slowed her steps and turned to us.

I knew her. I mean, I had seen her a few times at school. But I would never have recognized her. Her hair . . . well, it's light brown with gold streaks, and she used to wear it wild and free. Now it was bundled into a wispy braid. She was wearing thin round glasses, and she had dark circles under her eyes.

"Bailey Salinger?" Kate frowned. "What are you doing here?"

"Just scoping out the campus," Bailey explained.

"Really?" Kate took a breath and gazed around as if she had to be reminded where she was. "Don't tell me you're thinking about transferring in?"

"Yeah, sure," Bailey teased. "Like they'd take me. I wasn't the class brain like you, Kate."

She ducked her head. "I wish. I mean, maybe in high school. But here . . . I don't know. Everything's different."

"Yeah, it's like forty times the size of our high school," Bailey joked. "And you don't have your parents breathing down your neck."

A rueful expression darkened Kate's eyes. She started to say something, then stopped. "I—I'm late. I have to meet my tutor," she said, edging away. "A tutor! Can you believe it? I've got a killer integral calculus class. If I don't get my grades up, I'm going to flunk it."

"You'll be fine," Bailey called after her as she hurried away. Then he gave me a puzzled look. "Man, she looks wiped. And what was that about flunking calc? I mean, she was only the math whiz at Grant High School."

"Sounds like she's having a tough time here," I said. I remembered Kate graduating from high school with all these awards and scholarships. I always thought she was just like me.

Was Stanford going to do that to me, too?

No. No way. I just don't get bogged down and stressed out like that, I thought. I'm tough. Definitely tougher than Kate Fordham.

I followed Bailey into a bookstore, one of those places on campus where you want to grab a book and a cup of coffee and camp out on one of the sofas for a day or so. I was leafing through a fat collection of eighteenth-century poets, when Bailey popped up and flashed some cards in my face.

"Stationery," he said, handing them to me. They were old-fashioned postcards with cheesy sayings like GREETINGS FROM STANFORD! "You can write home with important messages. *Send food. Send cookies. Send money.*"

I nodded. "Works for me. Though the phone is faster." I picked out the funniest postcard and addressed it to Griffin, who was probably somewhere near Australia now.

It may sound weird, but I still felt really close to him, even though he was on the other side of the world and I'd started seeing someone else. There was no one here who knew me as well as Griffin did. No one that made me feel so . . . at home.

So I kept sending letters off to him. It felt right. Even if he didn't write back all that often.

Remember how you teased me about my twenty-year plan? I wrote. Well, here I am, Stanford bound. And it feels pretty great. So . . . make fun of me all you want. But come September I'll be starting Step One of the plan.

Chapter 2

So?" Claudia looked up from the kitchen counter, where she was doing her homework. "How was it? Did you like it?"

Bailey rooted around in the refrigerator while I sorted through the mail. "It was nice," I said.

"Nice? *Nice!*" Claudia protested. "A trip to your future university . . . Mom's alma mater . . . and all you can say is *nice?*"

"I'm not in yet," I pointed out. And from sifting through the mail, I could see that my college status hadn't changed. No answer from Stanford.

What were they waiting for? Was there something wrong with my application? I wondered nervously.

Or—was there a chance I hadn't gotten in?

No. No way! I *had* to get into Stanford. I'd never even seriously considered going anywhere else.

I'm in, I told myself. The letter is late, that's all.

Charlie walked in and nearly slammed into Bailey, who was backing away from the refrigerator door.

"You meeting us for dinner tonight?" Charlie asked Bailey. Once a week we all meet at Salinger's to touch base.

"Unh-unh. Busy." Bailey hoisted the milk carton to his mouth.

"Bailey," Claudia moaned. "You're supposed to be there."

"I can't help it," Bailey insisted. He unwrapped something from the fridge—a leftover tamale, I think—and bit in.

"Way to go, Bay. Why don't you go home and raid your own refrigerator?" Charlie asked.

Bailey swallowed, then answered, "It's empty." He peered into the fridge again. "Got any beer?"

"Isn't it a little early to start drinking?" I asked.

"Hey, it's past noon. Anyhow, I need to drown my sorrows after seeing Stanford. I mean, how am I ever going to be happy at San Francisco State again?" Bailey demanded. "I'll be so jealous thinking of you down the pike in paradise."

I couldn't help laughing. Bailey was so sure of me. It made me feel sure of *myself.*

The letter would come. And then my life would get rolling.

Later that afternoon, I was stretched out at the Coffee House, my head on the overstuffed arm of the sofa, my feet propped up on Sam's knees.

There's something about the Coffee House, I don't know what, but it's easy for me to unwind there. Low music and quiet voices and the smell of coffee.

Somehow they all blend together to make this really relaxing atmosphere.

And did I mention that I was stretched out across my boyfriend's lap? And did I mention that Sam was, well, gorgeous?

Sure, he was fun to be around, too. But he was one of those guys who had this ability to make your heart race with one flash of his blue-green eyes. He had brown hair, streaked from the sun. And because he spent so much time doing physical labor, he was really muscular. I mean, the first time I saw Sam barechested on a job site . . . well, that won me over.

I met him when he was hired to repair our roof. He had his own business renovating houses. He was pretty successful for a guy in his early twenties.

I'd never gone out with someone that much older than me before. So far it was really different from all my other relationships. Slower. Calmer. Like, we weren't sleeping together yet, even though we'd been seeing each other for over a month. I wasn't ready, and Sam wasn't pushing. It wasn't one of those burning-passion things like I had with Griffin.

But it was fun. I liked the lightness of it.

"So I told the guy that I couldn't get to his house for a while, but he just didn't want to hear it," Sam said, describing this estimate he'd done that day. "'I'm right in the middle of a big job,' I told him. 'It's a Tudor, and it's complicated.'" Sam's eyes danced. "'A two-door?' he says. 'So what's the big deal? My place has two doors, too. One in front, and one in back!'"

I giggled. "How did you not crack up right in his face?"

"I had to bite the inside of my cheek," Sam

admitted. He reached over and started to rub my bare ankles. "So how did it go at Stanford?"

"Okay, I guess."

"That good, huh? Your enthusiasm is knocking me over."

"It's not that bad," I admitted. "I mean, Stanford was really exciting. But the waiting is killing me. You know, my friend Libby already heard from Harvard. She's in! Case closed. I wish I could be so lucky."

"You are," Sam said. He picked up my hand and kissed the inside of my wrist lightly. "After all, you've got me."

"You know what I mean," I said. "Every application takes forever, with essays to write. And you have to bug your teachers to send your recommendations in on time. And then you can bet that some admissions officer is going to look at your application and find this major flaw with your life. Like, *Julia Salinger: Not enough extracurricular activities.*"

Sam moved his hands over my knees and massaged my calves. "Hanging at the Coffee House doesn't earn you bonus points?"

"Not quite," I murmured. His hands felt so good! I closed my eyes and took a deep breath, riding the wave of feeling. I thought about asking if he wanted to go someplace more private. But I felt too good to move. For a second, the rest of the world was fading out, getting rubbed away.

Just for a second . . .

"Julia."

I opened my eyes to see my friend Justin. He was standing a few feet away, looking awkward and weird. "Can I talk to you?"

"Yeah, sure." I sat up. What was up with him? I

wondered. I mean, he and I used to date, but that was a long time ago. We'd both moved on. He couldn't be weirded out by seeing me with Sam. Could he?

"This is Sam, by the way," I said quickly. "Sam, Justin."

They nodded at each other, but Justin obviously wasn't in a social mood. And as he motioned me to the corner, I could see that his eyes were red and sort of panicky. *Oh, no. He must have gotten a major rejection,* I thought. *Maybe from Yale.*

"Be right back," I told Sam as I slipped on my clogs and followed Justin. *It's not that bad,* I thought, planning what to say to Justin. *You'll get into another school. A better school.*

It sounded okay, but the shaky feeling inside me told me it was lame. It was as if rejection were some awful contagious disease.

Suddenly, Justin grabbed my wrist and pulled me close to the counter. "So you didn't hear yet."

"Hear what?"

"I heard it through Gail," he said breathlessly, "because Gail's mother and Libby's mother are friends and—"

He was making me nervous. "What are you talking about?"

"Libby's dead," Justin blurted out.

"That's ridiculous," I said blankly. I couldn't process it. What did he mean, Libby was dead?

"She's dead, Julia," Justin whispered. "She killed herself."

Chapter 3

The rest of the day ran together like that ugly brown blur that Owen gets when he mixes all his watercolors together.

I remember holding on tight to Justin. Kind of like we were keeping each other from sinking down into this awful place. "Oh, my God," I kept saying, again and again. "Oh, my God."

I remember Sam driving me home. Telling me things would be okay. Telling me how sorry he was.

I remember standing in the kitchen and staring at the phone and thinking about how I had owed Libby a call.

I was stunned. Almost numb.

Why? I kept asking myself. Why did she do it?

No one knew any of the details. No one could tell me why Libby killed herself. I mean, I knew that nothing could bring her back, but somehow it seemed

like we could all get some . . . I don't know . . . *relief,*
if we just understood what had happened. But I didn't
know where to begin.

That night I sat at our table at Salinger's and stared
at the full bread basket. It was hard to swallow
anything because of the thick feeling in my throat.

"How did Libby—" Claudia began. "I mean,
what—"

I knew what she was asking. "She took pills," I told
her. "Sleeping pills, I think. And then she went into
the garage."

I paused, twisting my napkin in my fingers. "I never
called her back. I was supposed to. I just didn't get
around to it."

Claudia's brown eyes were sympathetic. "You
should have called her," she admitted. She broke a
roll in half and handed a piece to Owen. "You should
have called. But people do that all the time. Forget to
return calls. You can't blame yourself."

"But maybe I could have helped her," I murmured.

Claudia didn't have an answer for that. She just
chewed on a roll and swallowed while I fell into this
whole guilt thing.

The truth is, Libby and I weren't really close. At
least, not lately. We'd been tight when we were kids,
but in the past few years we'd drifted apart. There was
never an argument or anything like that. It was a
subtle thing.

And now I felt guilty about that. Maybe if we'd
stayed close . . . if I'd been there for her . . .

God. Suddenly I had this intense longing to talk to
Griffin. Griffin could help me make sense of it all.

But Griffin wasn't here. He was ten thousand miles away.

I was making myself crazy. But I couldn't leave it alone.

That's how I found myself staring at the house I used to know well, the house where Libby Dwyer had lived. It was almost nine o'clock, kind of late to just go knocking on the door. But then again, would the Dwyers be sleeping tonight? I mean, when one of your kids—you know, does that, do you ever do anything normal again?

Still feeling awkward, I stood on the front stoop and pressed the doorbell. The waiting was torture.

Then the door opened and Mrs. Dwyer looked at me.

"Julia," she said, almost smiling for a second. Then her face crumpled. She reached out and hugged me. "Please, come in."

It felt strange walking into the Dwyers' house again—sort of like stepping back in time. We stood in the living room, still so neat you could see the vacuum tracks on the floor, and faced each other awkwardly.

"Is there—is there anything I can—" I stammered.

"No. . . ." Mrs. Dwyer shook her head. Tears began to form in her eyes again. She turned away and took a deep breath.

"Well . . . maybe . . . maybe there is," she added suddenly. "Here."

She started down the hall and I followed, noticing the stillness in the house. It reminded me of the time when my parents died. Everybody moped around and whispered under their breath. I don't understand why people do that. They either tiptoe around you or avoid you entirely. But for me it felt like a time for noise. You know, street traffic and rock music and booming voices . . . anything to drown out the pain.

We ended up in Libby's bedroom, where Mrs. Dwyer opened the closet.

"There are some clothes—some sweaters we got her for Christmas. She never even . . ." She pulled out an ivory sweater and held it up to my chin. "See? This would look pretty on you."

The whole idea of wearing Libby's stuff made me really uncomfortable, but I just nodded, trying not to hurt her mom's feelings. "Okay," I said. "Um—thanks."

Mrs. Dwyer sat down on the bed, her shoulders starting to shake. "What am I going to do?" she gasped. "I don't know what to . . . how was she . . ." Suddenly she was sobbing hard, barely able to talk. "Why didn't we know?"

"Nobody knew," I told her. "All of her friends thought she was okay. Happy."

"I wish she'd left a note. Something. Or maybe I don't."

I took a seat beside her and watched her cry, not knowing what to do. Should I put my arm around her? Get her some water? Just let her sob?

Then I realized that I was sitting on Libby's bed—the way I had years ago. We used to huddle there and laugh and tell each other stories and read funny sections from her journal.

But that would never happen again. *God, Libby,* I wanted to say. *What was so terrible that you had to kill yourself?*

With a deep breath, Mrs. Dwyer got quiet again. She squeezed my hand. "Thank you for coming, Julia."

I looked around the room once more. Then it hit me.

"You know," I said softly, "she had a journal."

Mrs. Dwyer's eyes widened. She looked almost frightened.

"I mean, she did when we were kids," I added. "It's been a while. But maybe she still—"

"Do—do you know where she kept it?" Mrs. Dwyer asked.

"Under the bed," I said. "In the box from her cowboy boots." Isn't it weird, the details that stick in your head?

Mrs. Dwyer reached under the bed and slid the box out. It was there, just as I remembered it, a red leather journal with a pen clipped onto it. Libby's mother held it in her hands for a moment.

At last she gave a little shudder. "I can't," she murmured, and handed the diary to me. "I can't read it now. Please . . . take it. Maybe—maybe someday . . ."

My fingers closed over the worn red leather, and I nodded. I understood. She was already in so much pain. She couldn't stand any more.

But *I* couldn't stand not knowing.

Holding tight to Libby's journal, I folded up a couple of sweaters that I didn't want. I hugged Mrs. Dwyer and said good-bye.

I tried to stay calm, hold back till I got home. But as I tossed the sweaters on the passenger seat and slid behind the wheel, my pulse seemed to be roaring in my ears.

I couldn't wait another minute.

Her journal. The answer had to be there. I closed the car door and gently opened the book. Libby's tiny, looped handwriting stared up as I smoothed back the pages.

Systematically, I read through the entries, starting with the ones dated back in November, more than two months ago.

Ninety-four on the calculus test, she wrote. *Dummy!*

I smiled. Libby was always hard on herself. Once she got mad at me when I told her she was a perfectionist. She gave me the cold shoulder for a few days. Then she admitted I was right, and we had a good laugh over it when she turned around and tried to reorganize my locker.

Then there were a few entries about Harvard. *I can't even think about not getting in,* she wrote. *I'd die. I would.*

I recognized that pressure. We were all feeling it.

I scanned ahead. I was getting close to the final entry—the last time Libby wrote in her diary.

She wrote some more stuff about Harvard after she got accepted. She mentioned being afraid that she would fail there.

Libby fail? Not very likely, I thought.

Then I realized I'd reached the end. There was one more line. This had to be it. The reason. The answer.

I read the words breathlessly. Then I read them again, frowning this time.

I'm never going to be one of them.

That was it? Libby's last entry?

I stared into space, holding the diary in my hands. "I don't get it," I muttered.

It didn't explain anything at all.

Chapter 4

I still don't get it," I told Justin.

We were sitting in my room, trying to piece together what Libby might have been thinking. "I mean, I've read this over a million times and it still doesn't explain anything."

"Maybe sometimes there isn't one big reason to kill yourself," Justin said, his voice hoarse.

I felt awful for him. Nobody was hit harder than Justin. He felt kind of responsible because he and Libby had gone out a while ago. He'd moved on—but maybe she hadn't.

I opened Libby's diary to the page with the final entry. Maybe Justin could figure it out.

"This is the last entry she wrote," I explained, reading:

"I got accepted to Harvard today. 'Dear Libby Dwyer, welcome to Harvard.' I feel like somebody

dropped a million-pound weight on me and it's crushing me. Why did I want this? Who was I kidding? What if I screw up?"

"Whoa." Justin shook his head in disbelief. "That doesn't sound like Libby. She was so focused on Harvard."

I nodded. "I know. Weird, huh? And there's more. Listen to this: *How am I going to pass these courses? Oh, God, if I flunk out, that's worse than not getting in. I can't do this. And I look at those pictures in the catalogue—all those kids who are smarter than me and better than me and more popular than me."*

I took a deep breath, then added, "And this. This is the very last line. *I'm never going to be one of them."*

Justin blinked back tears. "That's it? There's no more?"

"Do you get it?" I demanded. "Does it tell you why?"

He shook his head.

"I mean, didn't she know she had nothing to worry about?" I felt as if my voice were going out of control. "Libby was pretty, she was really smart, she—I just want to understand!"

Justin covered his face with his hands.

And we sat there. Silent. Wondering.

Scared.

"None of us knew that Libby was in pain," Gail Vogel said. She paused dramatically to look over at the coffin.

I blinked, feeling my stomach twist as Gail droned on. Her voice was annoying. No, maybe it was her whole act. I mean, she was supposed to be Libby's friend, but somehow I felt as if I were watching a really bad audition for the school play.

I took a deep breath and tried to focus on something else. There were a lot of familiar faces in the crowd. Justin was there, pale and shaky. Attendance at the funeral was impressive. It made me think of something Libby wrote in her journal.

All those kids who are smarter than me and better than me and more popular than me . . .

"You're pretty popular now," I wanted to say.

God, it was awful.

I tuned in to Gail again. "And if she could come back and say one thing to us, I know what it would be," Gail was saying. "It would be, don't stop your lives over this. I mean, she'd want us to remember her, definitely. But Libby was the kind of person who'd want us to keep going."

Oh, please. It was such a pat speech. Keep going? That wasn't what Libby said in her diary. Not at all.

As I sat there, things suddenly began to click into place in my mind. Or—maybe not in my mind. More in my heart. My guts.

Gail had it wrong . . . all wrong. She didn't have a clue.

But I did.

As Gail walked back to her seat, I moved to the podium. I caught Justin's startled glance out of the corner of my eye.

Staring out at the sea of faces, I cleared my throat. This was totally nerve-racking. I knew that some people wouldn't want to hear what I had to say. But I had to say it anyway.

"Um . . . I don't . . . I don't think Gail is right."

Silence. Gail's head whipped around. She blinked at me as if I'd just slapped her.

Steeling myself, I went on. "I don't know if Libby would say, 'Keep going.' I kind of think she would say, 'Stop.' Stop and make sure that the stuff you're doing right now—right now—is really what makes you happy. You know?"

The faces in front of me were a blur as I tried to keep cool. Tried to find the words.

"I'm trying to find something to take from this. Because otherwise, all it is is that my friend is dead, and that's . . ."

Justin suddenly hunched over as if he'd been punched, and I had to stop for a second. Man, this was hard.

"The thing is, you can't just live for some goal in the future and have that be everything. That's what Libby did."

I tried to make out faces in the crowd, but I couldn't see beyond the tears that stung my eyes. Did they understand? Were they getting it? I had to make them understand that Libby reached for a goal that just didn't deliver. It wasn't enough.

It wasn't a life.

"It's like she got on this road. And there were all these signs—THIS WAY, THIS WAY. But what if you get there, what if you get exactly what you wanted—like Libby did—and you find out that all the things that were wrong are still wrong? Then what?"

I looked at the casket covered with white flowers.

"God, Libby," I whispered. "I'm sorry you were so unhappy. I'll miss you."

* * *

My friend was buried today, I wrote to Griffin. *She killed herself because she was scared. Too scared to go on.*

I'm starting to wonder if maybe I should be scared, too.

I wish you were here.

Stretched out on my bed, I kicked off my shoes and chewed the end of my pen. A bunch of people went to the Coffee House after the funeral, but I just came home. Gail said we should be together, but somehow it didn't feel right. I didn't want to be with them. The only person I felt like talking to was Griffin.

But I couldn't. So instead, I was writing him this letter.

I thought about the last time we were together, about the way he'd joked about my twenty-year plan. Yeah, he teased me about it, but underneath all that, I thought, Griffin sort of likes that part of me. The Big Plan.

Only now I was wondering . . . maybe there were some flaws in the plan.

I was feeling this pressure, the crushing weight that Libby had written about.

What if I screw up? I wrote. *I mean, it doesn't end with getting into Stanford. I could flunk out.*

Or I could do fine, but hate what I end up becoming.

I shuddered. That was a scary thought.

I could be on the wrong road.

Just like Libby.

Chapter 5

"Marching here and there. Marching everywhere!" Owen chanted. He was stomping his feet in front of the television, singing along with a cartoon character. He had a huge grin on his face and a cereal bowl on his head.

Then it was time to spin. His arms went wide and the cereal bowl went flying.

"Careful," I warned, though I couldn't help smiling. Owen was walking proof that life doesn't stop. Well, at the moment he was spinning, flying proof.

A few days had passed since Libby's funeral, but I still felt kind of unsettled about everything. Sort of like my secure, stable life had just vanished. I kept telling myself that things would be okay—that I'd get back on track as soon as I heard from Stanford and settled my college plans.

Otherwise, I'd sort of been on autopilot. But nothing jolted me into the moment like a Saturday morning with Owen. *Jolted* being the operative word.

I mean, he insisted on getting up at seven. It wasn't even noon, and already we'd dug up the backyard, made pancakes shaped like bears, and sung along with an orange kangaroo. Now he was lugging a heavy bag of blocks out of the toy chest.

"What now? You want to build something?" I asked.

"I got blocks!" He hoisted the bag, and a bunch of wooden blocks bounced onto the rug. Owen grinned.

"Okay," I said, sitting cross-legged on the floor. "Let's see. Do you want to build a castle?"

He wrinkled his nose. "Build a truck."

"How about a house?" I suggested.

"A truck."

"You build a truck. Here's some wheels." I picked out four round blocks and handed them to him. "I'm building a house."

First, I made a tall stack of thin blocks with a cylinder on top. "Here's a tower," I explained to Owen. "You can climb up here anytime you want. And it's so tall, you can see as far as you want. You can even see the ocean. See?"

He nodded. "Can we go to the beach?"

"Not right now," I said, building another wing. "And look at this big door. It's extra big so that lots of friends can fit through it."

"Umm-hmm." He pouted a little. "What about the truck?"

"We'll build a big garage for your truck. Here you go." I stacked up more blocks until Owen gave me a nod of approval.

"And you know what else?" I felt inspired. "We'll

put a sandbox in the backyard." I built a small square of blocks with two benches, and Owen shredded a tissue and put it inside for pretend sand.

I sat back and smiled. "Wow! Look what we built."

"Wow!" he echoed.

"What do you think, buddy?" I said. "Do I have a future in design? Or maybe architecture?"

Owen gave me an angelic smile.

Then he lunged forward and crashed into our project, scattering blocks under tables and chairs.

Is that a sign or something? I wondered as I chased him across the room.

That afternoon it was Charlie's turn to watch Owen. I headed over to Bailey's apartment to see what was going on. I hadn't seen him all week, which was kind of unusual.

But there was no answer. I knocked again and pressed the bell.

Nothing.

I had just turned away, when the door opened.

"Hey," Bailey said, rubbing his eyes. "It's a little early to be playing the bongos on my door, Jule."

"Hey, yourself." I pushed past him into the apartment. It was dark, but even with the shades down I could see the mess. Pizza boxes. Empty cans. Newspapers and wrinkled clothes. "It's a gorgeous Saturday afternoon, and this place looks like a cave."

He pulled down his T-shirt, and I realized that he'd just rolled out of bed. "It's home."

"Maybe for Neanderthals," I said. "Where's Callie?" Callie was his roommate.

Bailey shrugged. "Out. Somewhere."

"Anyway, what happened to you? I didn't see you at the funeral."

"Yeah, well, I didn't really know Libby that well."

"Bay, you've known her for years," I protested. "Don't tell me that's your only excuse."

"Whatever," he muttered. That's Bailey's way of saying that he doesn't want to discuss it. Sometimes he really ticks me off.

I cleared off a chair and sat down. "Want to get lunch?"

"Can't do it," he said, stretching out on the couch. "I'm tight on cash. Besides, I'm beat."

"Well, I'm glad this wasn't a wasted trip," I muttered.

"Give me a break." He rubbed his eyes. "You know, you could help me out here. Get your boyfriend to throw me some work."

"Sam? I can talk to him about it." It wasn't a bad idea. Sam was always hiring guys to work a day here and there. "I'll see if he's got something that works with your class schedule."

"Yeah," Bailey said. "I'd love a good reason to cut lit." He pulled a book off the coffee table and sat up. "Hey. Did you ever read 'The Love Song of J. Edgar Prufrock'?"

I smiled. "It's J. *Alfred* Prufrock. And the poem sounds nice. But Eliot was a woman-hater."

"Really?" He squinted. "How did you figure that? I mean . . . you really click into this stuff. You belong at Stanford, Jule."

I sighed. "I don't know," I said. "I mean, all the stuff with Libby and everything. I used to feel like I knew where my life was going. I sort of took stuff for granted. Now . . . I don't know. I'm not so sure. It makes you wonder."

"Yeah."

I sat back and stared up at the cracked ceiling of Bailey's apartment. "I mean, is there anything that *really* matters? With everything you plan, all the things you think you want to do in life . . . how can you know if your plan is right for you?"

"Whoa, Jule," Bailey mumbled. "Sounds like you're selling life insurance."

"Seriously. I'm really starting to question stuff. Like, do I really want to write? Or buy a house and have kids? Maybe I should just pick up and travel around the world. Or maybe I should do something to help people, like join the Peace Corps."

"Yeah." Bailey propped a pillow under his head. "Whatever."

"Think about it. This is me, Julia Salinger. I'm smart. I'm a reasonably deep person. How did I get through seventeen years without ever really questioning the path I was on?"

"Hmm." Bailey sounded thoughtful.

I sat up straight. "Do you ever wonder, Bay? Do you ever just wake up and question everything you ever planned? As if you're suddenly living this brand new life? With . . . like, endless possibilities?"

He didn't say anything. I looked at him for a reaction.

His eyes were closed.

"Bailey?"

The only answer was his steady breathing. I noticed the line of empty beer cans on the coffee table and sighed.

Bailey was out of it. My guess was, he was hung over.

Just when I was hitting on the stuff that really mattered.

I slammed my boots to the floor and stood up.

"Gee, thanks, big brother," I said, heading for the door. "Thanks for listening."

Chapter 6

So—you seeing him tonight?" Charlie asked. He stood in the doorway of my room that Saturday night, his arms folded across his chest. He reminded me of a prison guard.

"I'm going out with *Sam,*" I answered, putting my hairbrush down on the bureau and turning toward him. "You can say his name, Charlie. You won't choke or anything."

"Can't be too sure about that," he muttered.

"Would you back off?" I said. "I know what I'm doing."

"Do you?" he demanded, his eyebrows going up. "This guy isn't right for you, Jule. It's not just that he's older. He's all wrong. Sam never went to college. He's a blue-collar kind of guy. And I hate to see you getting in too deep with—"

"Don't say it, Charlie," I snapped. "You may be my big brother, but you can't live my life for me. Okay?"

He ducked downstairs then, but not soon enough. The whole scene made me bristle. And the problem with Charlie is that you can fend him off for a while, but he keeps coming back. Persistent. That's Charlie.

He's only a few years older than I am, I thought. What's with the wise-older-statesman act? He always tries to make me feel like a little girl.

Sam was almost the same age as Charlie. But he didn't do that to me. When I was with Sam, I felt like a different person. Sort of cool. Adult. Independent.

It was a very good feeling.

"All right! It's Saturday night," Sam said. He handed me a glass of mineral water and dropped some bills on the bar.

I turned to Abby and Henry, two of Sam's friends, and we all clinked glasses.

It felt good to be out on a Saturday night, away from the usual chaos of home, away from my friends who couldn't seem to talk about anything besides Libby and college these days.

Here, the music was loud and everyone kept laughing. No one talked about school stuff. They were all grown-up and living their grown-up lives.

Sam sneaked up behind me and slipped an arm around my waist. I nodded at Abby, who was in the middle of a story.

"So anyway," Abby continued. "There I was with a flat tire in the middle of Compton. A horrible neighborhood. I'm starving. No cash. Only a bank check."

"A check for seventy grand!" Henry added. "We'd just sold the house! She'd just left the closing."

"So what do I do?" Abby asked dramatically. "I walk right into this barbecue joint. I order up a platter of baby backs, and ask if they can break a check for seventy thousand dollars."

Everyone laughed.

"Good choice!" Sam said. "Those people make the best ribs."

Those people? I turned to him. "What does that mean?"

But my question was lost in the commotion as Henry went on. "Wait, wait! The story gets better! Then I show up to pay for the tow truck and the ribs. I slap down my credit card, but it turns out it expired the day before!"

Henry screwed up his face in the clownish way that usually made me crack up. But this time I didn't laugh. Sam's comment was still bothering me.

I waited for a break in the conversation, then turned and spoke quietly in his ear. "What did you mean when you said that?" I asked. "About 'those people' making good ribs?"

He shrugged. "It was a joke."

"But 'those people' . . . you meant African Americans?"

He nodded warily.

"And so . . ." I frowned. "It's a joke about how blacks are . . . what? Good cooks?"

"You're reading into things," he said.

"But you said 'those people.'"

He put his hands on his hips. "What's your point? That I'm racist? Because I'm not. I've got . . . like, three black guys working for me." He shook his head. "Boy, is this a date or an inquisition? I thought you liked to laugh."

"I do," I said, forcing a smile. "I guess I just . . . some things aren't funny."

"You're right," Sam said. He leaned down to kiss me, his eyes sparkling in the dim light of the bar. "You're always right. It's this annoying habit you have. But I'm working on it."

"You two ready to go?" Henry asked, glancing from Sam to me.

"Go?" I blinked. "Go where?"

"We thought we'd take the boat out," Abby said. She zipped up her jacket. "We keep it docked down at the marina, but most of the time it's such a waste. We never get to use it."

The boat? This was the first I'd heard of it, but I wasn't totally surprised. I mean, since Sam's friends had real jobs, they had the money to spend on things like hockey tickets, ski trips, cars, and boats. That was another difference between Sam and the high school guys I used to go out with.

"We're going to see the lights of San Francisco from the water," Henry said, gesturing at an imaginary skyline. "Who knows? Maybe we'll even stay to see the sunrise on the water."

I nearly choked on my mineral water. "Really?"

"What's the matter?" Henry teased. "You turn into a pumpkin at midnight?"

Sam and I exchanged a look. "Not at midnight," I murmured.

I mean, I didn't have an exact curfew or anything. But I could just imagine Charlie's reaction if I stayed out all night with Sam and his friends.

"Don't worry, Cinderella," Sam whispered in my ear. "I'll get you home before Charlie calls the cops."

Smiling, I slipped on my leather jacket. I was glad he was so quick to understand. It made me feel good.

But I would have felt even better if I didn't have to worry about Charlie in the first place.

Next Friday, when I walked into the house after school, I could tell immediately that something was up.

First of all, everyone was in the kitchen, whispering. Charlie was home from the restaurant. Owen was bobbing up and down like a toy boat. And Bailey was there in the middle of the day. These days, we usually didn't see him before dark—and not much then.

Something was definitely going on.

"Hey," I said, "what are you guys—"

"It came, Jule," Charlie announced with a huge grin.

"And it's thick," added Bailey.

"Yeah." Claudia lifted a fat envelope from the kitchen table. "Too thick to hold up to the light." She handed it to me and I saw the return address and the familiar seal.

Stanford University.

I gasped. *Thin letter—rejection. Fat packet—acceptance.*

It was thick. Really thick. Could it be . . . ?

"Congratulations!" Owen shouted.

"Hold off a minute, Owe," Charlie said, picking him up.

"Go on," Claudia said, prodding me. "Open it!"

This is it, I thought. Everyone seemed to be holding their breath as I tore open the envelope.

Claudia tried to read over my shoulder. "Well . . . ?"

"What does it say?" Bailey demanded.

"'Dear Ms. Salinger,'" I read aloud. "'We are pleased to welcome you to Stanford University.'"

The room seemed to explode around me as I clutched the letter.

Bailey threw his hands in the air. "Yes! Yes!"

"Oh, my God!" Claudia exclaimed. "I knew you'd get in, Jule! This is so great!"

Charlie popped the cork on a bottle of champagne and Claudia lined up glasses on the counter.

"Now?" Owen asked, tugging on Charlie's shirt.

"Now," Charlie agreed, nodding.

"Congratulations!" Owen shouted.

I touched his head, smiling, then looked back at the letter.

Everyone was celebrating, really happy for me. I kept waiting for the thrill to wash over me, too.

This was it. The answer I'd been waiting for. Acceptance. *Acceptance.* I was supposed to feel elated. Ecstatic. My life had a set direction now.

But nothing happened. The good feelings never washed over me. I just stood there feeling strange. Sort of embarrassed. And weighed down.

Claudia handed me a glass of champagne. "Charlie's been chilling this in the vegetable drawer since last week."

"What can I say?" Charlie grinned. "I knew you'd make it."

"To Julia!" Bailey raised his glass high, and everyone joined in.

But as I looked from one beaming face to another, I got really uncomfortable. I mean, it didn't feel right. I wanted to be out of there.

"Guys—don't," I mumbled. "Please."

"Why not?" Charlie said. "This is an occasion. Here's to knowing what you want, going for it, and—"

"Blowing the competition out of the water!" Bailey added.

That made Claudia sputter, spitting out her drink. Then she held out her glass for a refill, and Charlie gave her a hard time about drinking at her age. And Bailey started complaining about his schoolwork.

And everyone just rolled on as if I weren't standing there all balled up with tension. As if everything were okay.

When it definitely was not.

I'd really believed that this acceptance letter would put my life back on track. That it would make me feel steady and secure again. But as the celebration went on around me, I started to feel worse and worse.

What's going on? I wondered.

What is wrong with me?

Chapter 7

That night, when Sam picked me up, I didn't even mention the letter. I was still sorting through things. Why in the world did such good news make me feel so awful?

We didn't have any definite plans, so we just drove around the city for a while, looping over hills and people-watching. Then Sam found an empty spot right near the Cannery. It's an old brick building on the Bay where they used to can fruit and things. Now it's full of boutiques and restaurants and food concessions. Anyway, he found a parking spot and we got out to walk around and get some fresh air.

The sun was just about gone and it was getting cold, but we didn't feel like going inside. So we got two lattes and settled onto a low brick wall with a really beautiful view of the bay and the Golden Gate Bridge. Sam slipped one arm over my shoulders and I leaned into him. I tried to shake the bad feeling I'd had since that afternoon.

"Let me ask you something," I said. "How did you decide that renovating houses was right for you? I mean, was it a plan? Or did you just fall into it?"

"Kind of both." He lifted the lid from his cup and lapped up some of the foam. "I fell into a lot of jobs. And when I realized they were wrong for me, I sort of fell out of them. Eventually I fell into the right gig."

"How did you know the other jobs were wrong for you?"

"I don't know. I just did. In my gut."

"Right, you're right," I murmured.

A gut feeling. Well, I knew what that was about. I was having either a major gut feeling or an attack of appendicitis. "Trust your gut," I said, trying out the words.

But what you do when your gut tells you something you don't want to hear? Something that could change your whole life?

Sam took a sip of coffee, then pressed the lid down. "Let me go out on a limb here and guess this isn't about me."

I hunched up my shoulders. "Yeah . . ."

Taking the letter from my pocket, I handed it over. He unfolded it and held it up to the light to read it.

"Whoa," he gasped. "Wait. Are you kidding me? This is great! This is . . ." His voice trailed off as he caught sight of my face. "Why do you look like you're going to throw up?"

"I don't know. I keep reading it, trying to feel great about it. But every time, my stomach . . . I think it's like one of those jobs that didn't work out for you."

"That's different. Those jobs were stupid. But this is something you want."

"Really?" My throat felt tight, and I put my coffee cup down on the wall, suddenly not into it. "When did I decide that? When did I weigh my options and say, yes, *college*. Never. It's just been *assumed*. By everyone. My family, my teachers. Me."

"Okay, okay," Sam said, backing off a little. "It's a heavy decision. Something to think through."

"Yeah . . ." I said again. I turned and stared out at the bay, watching the light on Alcatraz blink on and off.

The truth is, I realized suddenly, I've already thought this through. What else have I been doing for the last two weeks?

I knew what I had to do. The only thing that felt *right*.

And once I accepted it, everything fell into place.

I had made my choice.

And I felt better already.

I held on to my decision all that night and through the next day. Sometimes you just have to let things sit awhile. You know, the way a stew has to simmer. Some decisions need to age before they can survive the light of day.

Or the Salinger clan.

But that night, when I walked into the kitchen and Charlie hit me with a direct question, I decided it was time to test the waters. Claudia was off at a violin lesson, and Owen was out with Bailey, so we had the whole house to ourselves.

Lucky us.

"So, Jule," Charlie said as he stood at the counter

building a sandwich. "Is all your paperwork in order? All the records and stuff that you need for Stanford?"

"Well . . ." I put the juice carton back in the fridge and closed the door. "Not exactly."

"You need a check for a deposit? Because we can work out something for—"

"That's not it," I said quickly. "The thing is . . ." I took a deep breath. "The thing is, I'm not going, Charlie."

"You're *what?*" The mustard knife skittered onto the counter as he whipped around to stare at me. "Did you say you're not going to Stanford? Jule, that's not something to joke about."

"It's not a joke," I said. "And it's not something I feel like fighting about. College isn't . . . it's just not the right thing for me now."

"Hang on." Charlie held up both hands. "Can't we have a conversation about this? I mean, this is a huge decision. And I need to know what you're thinking."

I wanted to bolt out of there. A lot of times Charlie turns discussions into speeches. But at that moment he seemed to be trying really hard to be patient and listen. And I wanted to make him understand my decision.

"It's hard to describe," I began. "It's like—I'm tired of being me. The A student. Good old reliable Jule."

A sad expression lit his eyes. He was trying to understand—sort of. But I could tell that he wasn't getting it.

"It's sort of like . . . these . . ." I pulled one of Owen's drawings off the refrigerator and handed it to him. He had drawn a big red train that was chugging up a hill, past a brown cow.

"Remember when Mom used to hang our stuff up and you could always tell which one I did?" I asked. "Because you and Bailey, your clouds were purple and your skies were orange. But me—my drawings were always right. Blue skies, white clouds. By the book. Every single time."

Charlie pushed the drawing away, his brows knit with concern. "Julia, look. This is just a phase. Senior spring. Everyone goes through—"

"No, it's not," I insisted. He wasn't getting it. "It's about me. I need to find out who I am."

"So do that at college," he said, speaking softly. "And then, when you finish—"

"You're not listening to me!" I burst out. God, this was so frustrating! I should have known better than to try to explain anything to him. He would never understand. Never.

There was a knock on the back door, and from the corner of my eye I saw Sam step in. But I was too steeped in the argument to stop now.

"I can't just sit back and watch while you make a huge mistake," Charlie growled, his face turning red.

"I'm not making a mistake!"

"Whoa." Sam backed toward the door. "I'll wait outside."

"No, stay," I said, waving him in. "It's nothing you haven't heard."

That set Charlie off even more. He looked from Sam to me, suddenly suspicious. "You two have talked about this?"

I shrugged. "Yeah. So?"

"Oh, I get it." Charlie swung toward Sam, ready to attack. "So that's what this is about. This is about *him*. He's the one who put this idea in your head."

Anger boiled over inside me. "Charlie!"

"All I did was listen to her, Charlie," Sam said, holding up his hands defensively. "I never told her what to do."

"So then butt out!" Charlie shouted.

"Cut it out!" I marched over and stood between them, furious with Charlie and a little ticked at Sam. They were talking about me as if I were some little kid playing follow the leader. Someone incapable of making her own decisions.

"I'm serious, Sam," Charlie said through clenched teeth. "I don't want you in this house." He pointed at the door. "Get out."

A sick feeling hit me when Sam stepped forward, seething with fury. For a moment I thought he was going to punch Charlie.

Then he seemed to back off. "No problem," he growled sarcastically, then stormed out.

"Who the hell do you think you are?" I yelled at Charlie. I was furious. I knew Charlie wouldn't like my decision. I had expected his disapproval . . . but not this.

To imply that I had made this choice because some guy "put an idea in my head"! And that I couldn't make my own choices!

"You have no right—" I started.

"Sure I do," he cut in. "I'm your guardian. And if you go letting some guy screw up your life, it's *my* fault."

His fault! Like it didn't matter that it was *my* life!

There was no way I could reason with Charlie. How can you reason with a total tyrant? A tyrant disguised as a "guardian."

"Okay," I said. "So let me get this straight. You

don't care about me or my life. You just care about how my actions reflect on you." I let out a short laugh. "That's great! That's great parenting."

I grabbed my knapsack and went to the door. Charlie just stood there, shaking his head, as if to say: *Oh, you're so dumb, but you'll see . . . you'll see.*

"I'm sure Mom and Dad would really approve of this." I didn't even try to keep the bitterness out of my voice. I couldn't. "Way to go, Charlie."

Then I walked out, slamming the door behind me.

Chapter 8

After that Charlie and I avoided each other. Sort of like a cold war.

No one else knew why it was going on. But Claudia definitely knew something was up. She walked around with this spooked expression on her face. Even Owen could tell, I think. He was quieter than usual.

I felt bad for them—especially Claud. But I didn't want to talk about it. I mean, I was already totally confused about where my life was going. Advice from my little sister could only make things worse.

So I kept everything to myself for a few days. I typed out a letter to Stanford, telling them that I couldn't take the spot. And you know what? When I dropped it into the mailbox I felt good. Like I was free to live my life at last.

The next day when I was driving Claudia to school, I finally told her about my decision.

"Oh, wow. Wow. Is that what's been going on between you and Charlie?" she asked. "You don't talk. You won't even stay in the same room anymore."

"Charlie can't deal with the fact that I'm growing up," I said. "He wants to run my life. But he can't."

Claudia frowned. "So what are you going to do? You know, instead?"

"Get a job," I answered. "Maybe get a few jobs. Keep getting them till I find one I love."

"But what kind of job?" Claudia asked. "It's hard to find something good without a college degree. You know, something really interesting."

My fingers tightened on the steering wheel. Sometimes Claudia can really get to me—without meaning to.

"College doesn't guarantee anything, Claud," I pointed out. "Look at all the people who have great jobs without it."

"I don't know. I guess that works for some people. But you're not like that, Jule. You're such a—a *student.*"

I was getting sick of hearing that. "Well, I can't be a student for the rest of my life, can I?" I snapped.

"Hey, don't bite *my* head off," she said, hurt. She turned away and stared out the window. And the car was silent for the rest of the ride.

So much for family support.

That day I got a message during homeroom. It said that I should report to the guidance counselor's office to meet with Mrs. Huffman during third period. I had already told her I was turning down the Stanford offer. I assumed that this meeting was one of those formalities. You know, like a follow-up.

I was wrong.

She greeted me at the door with a bright smile. "Julia! Thanks for coming down. We want to discuss your options."

"We?" I frowned. "Who's—?"

Just then she swung the door open and I saw him sitting in a chair in her office.

"Charlie?" I froze in the doorway. "Oh, man."

He looked up with a smile that made my skin crawl. "Before you get mad at me, I just thought we should talk this out, okay?"

I felt betrayed. Totally ambushed! My instincts told me to get out of there.

But I stayed. I mean, what if I left and the two of them sat together and planned my future without me? That's just the sort of thing Charlie would do.

"So let's talk," Mrs. Huffman said. She closed the door and sat down. I perched on the edge of my chair, trying to prepare myself for a major inquisition.

"Obviously, things are a little—overwhelming for you now," Mrs. Huffman said, giving me a look that oozed pity. "It's probably not the best time to be making huge decisions like this. So the best solution, I think, is to defer for a year and then—"

"I told you," I snapped. "I don't want to defer."

"Why not?" Charlie jumped in. "Mrs. Huffman says all you have to do is write a letter that tells them how you're going to spend the year, and then—"

"That's kind of the point," I said. "I don't *know* how I'm going to spend the year."

"So make something up," Charlie said. "You're a

writer. Then you can take a year off, give it some time. And then, if you still don't want to go—that's okay. Fine. It'll be your decision."

I glared at him. "It's my decision now."

"Julia, look." Mrs. Huffman leaned forward. "I know it's been difficult for everyone after—what happened to Libby. It's confusing, I know. But your brother tells me you've been spending time with an older man who may have influenced—"

"Charlie!" I gasped, feeling as if I'd just been knocked off my feet. How could he? Did he really believe that Sam . . . and to tell Mrs. Huffman about him! "I can't believe you. This is not about Sam!"

"Oh, come on," Charlie said. "Ever since you've been hanging out with that guy—"

"Wow," I said quietly. "You've really got it in for him, don't you?"

Charlie was heating up, his face getting red. "Yeah, I do. Because he's a twenty-four-year-old *roofer* and you're seventeen and *obviously* he's not the most together person on the planet—"

Mrs. Huffman interrupted. "Let's try to discuss this—"

"—and he doesn't have a clue what's best for you!" Charlie finished, pointing at me accusingly.

"Oh, and *you* do?"

"Yeah, I do! And I'm not going to let you throw your future away because of some guy. So you're going to Stanford, or you're going to defer a year—because you know what?" he barked. "I'm the guardian. And as long as I'm in charge, and as long as you live in my house—"

"Your house!" I couldn't believe what I was hearing. Major power trip!

"—what I say goes!" Charlie announced like a king delivering a proclamation. "You got that?"

I was totally blown away. Blinded by anger, I sat there. What could I say? How could I fight?

The room was suddenly quiet as I looked over at Mrs. Huffman. She was no help. Just a paper-pusher.

That's when the will to resist drained out of me. I was beyond fighting. Beyond revenge. The only way I could survive was to find a way out of the stranglehold Charlie had on me. Otherwise I would shrivel up and die.

But for now, I was trapped. My only choice was to play Charlie's game.

With a super-sweet smile, I turned to my brother. "Wow, I guess you're the boss. So—what do you want me to do next?"

That afternoon, Mr. Langen took the class to the library so that we could start researching our history papers. I opened my notebook, but all the print just swam around. There was no way I could focus with Charlie's noose around my neck.

Instead, I started a new letter to Griffin. I hadn't heard from him for a while, but when he's on a ship it takes forever for his letters to get to me. I wondered how he liked Australia. I tried to picture him hanging out in Sydney harbor.

It sounded kind of cool, actually. Maybe I should do something like that. Take a long trip. See the world.

At least go somewhere away from Charlie.

I put my pen to the paper. Man, Griffin was going

to be surprised. A lot had changed since my last letter.

Just to bring you up to date, I wrote. *College is out. Freedom is in. Maybe you had the right idea when you sailed out of San Francisco. I'm not going too far. But I'm definitely cutting out.*

And I won't look back.

Chapter 9

As soon as school let out, I raced home. I blew into the house and ran up to my room. I pulled out the biggest suitcase I could find and began to throw clothes into it. It wasn't the most organized way to pack, but it was the fastest.

My goal was to get out of there before Charlie got home and staged another scene. Fortunately, he was working at Salinger's. Owen was in day care. Bailey hadn't been around lately.

That left just one obstacle—Claudia.

She intercepted me in the laundry room and followed me up the stairs with her usual rapid-fire questions. Sometimes I wish she would stay out of things that aren't her business.

"You can't just leave," she said. "You can't just go and—hey, don't take the hair dryer. What are *we* supposed to use?"

I rolled up a T-shirt and shoved it into the tumble of clothes. "Why is everybody so interested in telling me what I can't do?"

"What?" She squinted in confusion. "Julia, what's going on?"

Struggling to close the suitcase, I grunted, "Charlie says he's the boss as long as I live here. So, as of today, I don't live here." I heaved the suitcase up and dragged it into the hall.

"But—where are you going?" Claudia called, following me.

That brought me a moment of panic. Where *was* I going?

I thought about my friends. No good. Their parents wouldn't go for a runaway Salinger kid in their house.

I had to know somebody who was free. . . .

Then it came to me.

Sam!

"Hey!" Claudia called. "When are you coming back? And what about Owen? You're supposed to watch him this weekend. Julia!"

The suitcase thumped on each step as I lugged it down the stairs. I felt way too mad and way too crazy to answer any of Claudia's questions.

So I just stormed out.

Boy, was Sam surprised to see me. That night when he walked up the street swinging his toolbox, I was sitting on the steps of his apartment building with a bag of groceries. Sam paused. I think he was afraid he'd forgotten about an important date.

"I just thought I'd come make dinner for you," I said.

"Dinner." He frowned, sensing that something was a little off. "For me."

"Sure. And I got some videos for after that. And if we don't finish them tonight, we can watch tomorrow night."

"Tomorrow?" His eyes grew round.

"And the next night. And I brought some microwave popcorn. You have a microwave, don't you?"

He sighed. "What's this about, Jule?"

It was time to be honest. I owed that to Sam, especially considering the favor I needed. "Look, Charlie's ragging on me and I need to get away for a little while. And right now, this is about as far as I can go."

He shifted his feet, his heavy work boots scraping against the pavement. "I don't know, Jule. He already hates me."

I forced a smile. "So you've got nothing to lose, right?"

He shook his head. I knew what he was thinking. After all, the idea of a seventeen-year-old girl staying with a guy who's twenty-four . . . well, some people would freak.

Then Sam surprised me. Crossing his arms, he studied my face for a moment. "Okay," he said at last.

"Okay?" I blinked. "Great! Will you help me get my suitcase out of the car? It's kind of heavy."

"You came with a suitcase?" he asked. "You were that sure I'd say yes?"

I shrugged. "If you didn't, I'd have gone to Bailey's."

"Things are that bad with Charlie?" he asked.

I hoisted up the grocery bag. "Worse," I said.

* * *

Living with Sam was fun, even though I couldn't shake the feeling that I was on the run. I kept waiting for Charlie to show up at school or pop up at the grocery store.

But I tried not to think too much about Charlie and all the pressure he'd been trying to dump on me. Over the next few days I kept busy with my schoolwork, doing stuff around the loft, cooking for Sam.

He liked that. I mean, fresh pancakes beat instant oatmeal any morning of the week. And I don't think he minded when, one night when I couldn't sleep, I went through his pantry and reorganized and labeled and tossed out stuff that was way beyond edible. But I have to admit he got a little snappy when I suggested getting curtains.

One night I went to some major trouble to make a fancy dinner. A soufflé. I know, it sounds like one of those old *I Love Lucy* reruns. Only the soufflé turned out perfect—tall and fluffy. And with the lights lowered and candles flickering on the table, it didn't matter that Sam's glasses were mismatched or that the plates were chipped on the edges.

Then, just as we were about to sit down, the doorbell rang.

"I'll get rid of 'em," Sam called.

A minute later, I heard Claudia in the hallway.

"Claud?" I went out to the loft, trying not to give in to the panic that hit when I heard my sister's voice. "What's going on?"

Claudia shoved her hands into the pockets of her jacket. "Nothing. Except it was *your* day to watch Owen."

I took a breath. "Wait a minute. You came all the way here—at night—just to tell me that?"

Claudia flashed me a look of outrage, her hands on her hips. "Excuse me? Like I'm out of line for coming over here, when you're the one who's dumped everything on me so you could come here and play house."

That made my teeth grind. "Oh, give me a break, Claud. I mean, you couldn't just pick up the phone?"

"Sorry for putting you out. But I'm sick of getting stuck with everything while Bailey is gone and Charlie is busy with his new girlfriend, Grace. I'm fourteen years old, Julia. All the household stuff shouldn't fall on my shoulders."

"Well, you can thank Charlie—our *guardian*—for that," I said sarcastically.

"Hey, you two, I . . ." Sam looked really uncomfortable, sort of like a baseball was stuck in his throat. He grabbed his jacket. "I'm just going to go . . . somewhere else for a while."

"Stay, Sam," I insisted, grabbing his arm. "We're done here."

"No we're not!" Claudia snapped. "You can't just ignore all the stuff you have to do at home."

"I'll pull my weight, Claud," I told her. "But I'll do it from here. I'm not going back there."

"Whatever," she said. I tried to ignore the painful look in her eyes. "I'm going home."

"You want me to drive you?" Sam offered in a resigned voice. "It's late. And dark."

"I'll be okay," Claudia told us. "I took the MUNI."

"Claudia!" I wanted to scream. I mean, a kid her age riding public transportation alone at night! Meanwhile, I'd made this incredible dinner that would be ruined by the time Sam got back.

"Stay," I told her. "I'll drive you home after dinner." I turned to Sam, who looked like he still wanted to leave. "You don't mind, do you?"

"No," he said in a strained voice. "Why would I mind?"

Why? I thought as Claudia sat down at my artfully set table. Because my kid sister just crashed our romantic evening.

That's when I realized that there was no getting away from my family—not completely. The Salingers had a long reach. Like one of those cartoon octopuses with elastic arms.

Okay. So I had to take care of Owen occasionally. No reason that I couldn't do it at Sam's house.

The next day, when I picked Owen up from day care and drove over to Sam's, I was starting to feel good about the situation. I can make this work, I thought as I popped in a videotape and Owen's favorite orange kangaroo danced onto Sam's big-screen TV.

"Kooroo! Kooroo!" Owen clapped and twirled in delight.

"That's right," I told him. "You can see Kooroo lots of places. Even at Sam's house."

"Uh-huh," Owen said. His lollipop trailed over the upholstery as he pulled himself into Sam's favorite chair.

I opened my English notebook and started outlining a medieval ballad I was supposed to write. The time flew by as Owen played, and I whipped through two assignments.

When Sam blew in the door, I thought he'd be kind of tickled to see the way Owen had settled in. Instead, he yanked his keys out of the lock and nearly ripped off his coat.

"What's the big hurry?" I asked. "Something wrong?"

"I've got about thirty seconds."

"For what?"

"The Flyers and the Panthers. I blew off work so I could get home in time for the face-off and . . ." His voice trailed off as he stepped into the loft and noticed Owen. Owen, and Kooroo, the big orange kangaroo, hopping across his TV.

Sam's face fell. "Uh-oh."

"It's okay," I said quickly. "Owen? We have to turn Kooroo off now. Okay?"

Owen rolled over to peer up at us. "No."

"Really, Owen. It's Sam's turn to watch TV," I said firmly, feeling Sam's rising nervousness. "Remember how we share?"

"No! No! No!" Owen shouted, his face crumpling. "You promised!"

"Forget it!" Sam's hands flew up, as if he could wave off Owen's tears. "It's okay. I'll watch in the bedroom."

"On that little TV?" I said. "That doesn't seem—"

But Sam was already gone. And not very happy.

"We'd better get a hockey schedule so this doesn't happen again," I told Owen, who was busy turning somersaults in front of the television.

Oh, well. At least things were quiet.

But not for long. An hour or so later someone started pounding on the door. I mean, really pounding. It was so loud that it even brought Sam out of the bedroom.

I opened the door and Charlie stood there, clearly seething under a cool facade. He nodded at Owen, who was hammering away with his tool set.

"Hey, Owe," he said evenly. Then he turned and lashed out at me. "Were you ever going to call me back?"

"Hadn't planned to," I snapped. I made it sound casual, but inside I was a bundle of nerves. I knew this was going to happen. Showdown with Charlie.

"I'm sick of this," Charlie said. "You take off. You take Owen without leaving a note. You know what? I don't want him here at all. He's coming home. And you know what? You're coming, too."

"What? Listen to you! You're not my boss!"

"Charlie," Sam said, stepping between us. "Wait a minute—"

"You!" Anger flared in Charlie's eyes. "Butt out! My sister is seventeen and she's going home with me!" He spun toward me and barked, "Get your stuff, Julia. We're going."

"No. *You're* going!" I shouted. I couldn't take Charlie's attitude, barking commands as if I were a slave. I was burning with anger, so hot that all the words kind of jumbled together.

"I'm your legal guardian, Julia!" Charlie yelled.

"Guys—" Sam begged.

Then Owen burst into tears. A moment later Claudia showed up in the hall outside Sam's apartment.

"Nice work, guys!" She pushed past Charlie and bent down to pick up Owen. "It's okay," she told him.

I wanted to shout: *No! It's not okay! I'm trying to pull my life together and Charlie keeps ripping out the seams!* I held my hands to my head, trying to block out the sound of Owen's sobs.

"I'm not coming home!" I shouted.

Suddenly, the room went quiet. "I'm not," I repeated. "So just get out of here, Charlie."

His eyes were ablaze as he scooped up Owen and headed toward the door. Then he turned back. "I'm not done with this, Julia," he warned with a really hard look, and I knew it was true.

I hadn't seen the last of Charlie.

Chapter 10

I tossed and turned that night, feeling totally helpless. I mean, what can you do when you've got someone like Charlie over you, pushing buttons and pulling strings and trying to tell you what to do? And ultimately, at least legally, they're in charge.

It's totally unfair.

The next morning I was still plotting ways to get Charlie to back off. I was so focused on it that Sam took me by surprise when he served up a stack of pancakes.

"You cooked for me?" I smiled, tucking my robe around my legs. "This is so sweet."

He plunked down a bottle of syrup. "I just thought maybe I should do something nice. To counteract something not so nice."

That stopped my heart for a second. "Why am I

nervous all of a sudden?" I put my fork down and looked up at Sam. He was wringing his hands on a towel.

Yup. This was going to be bad.

"Look," he said. "First of all, I really like you, Julia."

I tried a smile. "That's not a good opener."

"The thought of living with you is . . . it's definitely tempting," he went on. "But it might be nice to try it when you're actually here because of me. Not because you're running away from home. From Charlie."

Running from Charlie.

Suddenly, the pancakes didn't look so appetizing.

"I know things are tough for you right now," he said. "But until you work it out, well . . . I've got a nice quiet little life going here. I come home. Watch a little TV. Listen to some music. I like it that way."

And you can't deal with the crazy Salingers spilling over into it, I thought.

My eyes met Sam's. "In other words," I said, trying to keep my voice light, "what you're saying is, you want me to get out of here."

"Exactly." His smile took some of the sting out of his answer.

Then he went into the kitchen. I sat there and thought for a minute. My emotions were all over the place.

First of all, I had to think about what Sam said. *I really like you.* Those were his exact words. Not *I love you* or *I'm crazy about you.*

Okay, so he wasn't in love with me. Well, I guess I kind of knew that. Just as I knew I wasn't in love with him.

The weird thing was, it wasn't the end of the world.

So we weren't in love. Maybe it would happen one of these days.

In the meantime, Sam did *like* me. He just couldn't protect me from my life.

I had to go home.

There wasn't any welcome-home party. No greetings. No marching band. I just lugged my suitcase up the stairs, bundled up my dirty clothes, and tossed them into the laundry room.

And that was that. I was home.

Sam and I were still seeing each other. And I was still waiting to see where our relationship was going.

Add to that a rotten home life. Things were so cold between Charlie and me that we might as well have lived in the North Pole. Not to mention the fact that Charlie's new girlfriend, Grace, was always around, butting into family business. I mean, she's an okay person. But who decided to make her part of the family? Charlie. The boss.

At least she wasn't invited to our family dinners at Salinger's. Although at the moment I'd be happy to let her have my place, I thought. I bit into a bread stick, buried my nose in a book, and tried to tune out the conversation.

Claudia was trying to discuss plans for Owen's birthday party without tipping Owen off. Owen was fidgeting in his seat. Charlie was shooting down most of Claudia's ideas. And Bailey—well, Bailey was late. As usual.

One thing I could count on during this whole crisis with Charlie was Bailey. That is, I could count on him *not* to be there. And when he did show up, he was always spacy and out of it. He broke up with Sarah, his longtime girlfriend, and started seeing Callie, his roommate. Sarah's a good friend of mine—I could tell she was really devastated. She told me that Bay spent too much time partying. She was worried there was something wrong with him.

All I knew was that he had disappeared from my life.

"I think we have . . ." Claudia counted up the guest list, "Twenty kids."

"Twenty's too many, Claud," Charlie said. "You have to cut it down."

"Cut what down?" Bailey asked, sliding into the booth beside me. I didn't even bother to look up at him. What was the point?

"What are you talking about?" he asked Claudia.

"The p-a-r-t-y list," she answered.

"What party?" Bailey asked.

"Yeah," Owen chimed in. "What party?"

"Bailey!" Claudia's dark eyes were furious as she leaned toward Owen. "Potty," she told him. "He said potty, Owe."

Charlie nodded toward Owen and spelled out the word *birthday*. "This Saturday," he added.

"Oh, right!" Bailey smacked his forehead. "Man, I totally forgot!"

"I'm stunned," I said in a flat voice. I mean, it's so annoying. Bailey acts like he's on top of things, but lately he barely knows what day it is.

Charlie winced. "Is it too much to ask that we have an attitude-free dinner?"

"Whatever you say." I gave him a wide, sickly sweet smile. "You're the boss."

"Could you two just stop for a minute?" Claudia

said. "We need to come up with a time when we can all get together."

"For what?" Bailey asked blankly.

"Duh. P-a-r-t-i-e-s don't just plan themselves. And this is something we can all do. You know, *together.*"

Silence. Bailey rubbed his eyes as if he were too tired to pick up his napkin, let alone plan a party. I glared at Charlie. Oh, this was going to be a blast.

"Look," Charlie told Claudia, "I'm really stretched for the next few days."

"But what about the c-a-k-e?" Claudia asked, trying to hide her disappointment. "And someone has to be home by three tomorrow to interview the c-l-o-w-n."

I snorted. "We have to interview clowns?"

"Julia!" Claudia gritted as Owen's head snapped around.

"Why don't we just divvy up the jobs and do them on our own time?" Bailey suggested.

"I'm all for that." I grabbed Claudia's list and scribbled my name next to the cake detail. Bailey signed up for the clown, and Claudia wrote her name next to "Decorations"—but not without a huge sigh. That left Charlie to buy the toys.

"Okay, great," Charlie said, handing the list back to Claudia.

But she just shook her head glumly, refusing to take it.

"What's the matter?" Charlie asked.

"I just—" Her voice cracked with emotion. "I really wanted us all to do something fun together for a change."

Bailey threw his arms out to encompass the restaurant. "What do you call this?"

But Claudia just shook her head, fighting tears. She was really disappointed. I guess she expected this party thing to be a real family fun thing. She didn't want to see the truth—that these days most of us couldn't stand to spend ten minutes in the same room with each other.

Claudia could miss the big picture at times. Still, I felt bad for her. So after we choked down our dinners, I made a point of spending some time with her. "You want to get a head start on those decorations?" I asked as we headed out to the parking lot.

She nodded. So we sent Owen home with Charlie and headed off to a big party store near Chinatown that's open till midnight.

I picked up a curled paper streamer. "These are cool," I said. "You just pop the top off and the streamer flies out."

Claudia frowned. "Yeah, but it might scare some of the kids. They're only three."

Sometimes I think Claudia is really somebody's old grandma trapped in a kid's body.

I walked down an aisle crowded with bins of paper toys. At the end was a row of Happy Birthday banners. "How about that one?" I pointed to a shiny banner with foil curlicues hanging down.

At last, she brightened. "Owen will like that."

We ended up buying two banners, napkins and plates decorated with Kooroo the Kangaroo, and a bunch of little toys to give away as favors. By the time we piled everything on the counter, Claudia's spirits had lifted.

"This is going to be his best party yet," she said confidently. Her brown eyes were serious for a moment as she looked up at me. "Thanks, Jule. For helping with this. It's funny, but Bailey is usually the one who . . . he usually makes things up to me. Tries to make me feel good. But he's never around anymore."

"Yeah," I said. "Let's hope he gets his act together for hiring the clown."

"Oh, he will," Claudia assured me. "Bailey would never let Owen down."

I nodded and pushed Bailey to the back of my thoughts. I had enough on my mind trying to dodge Charlie when we got home. Then there was school. And ordering Owen's cake.

The lady at the bakery showed me this little orange statue of Kooroo that they used on kids' cakes. It was really tacky, but I knew he'd like it, so I told her to go for it.

And then there was Sam. It isn't easy trying to fit someone into your life when he has a job and you're busy with school and family stuff.

Anyway, Sam and I decided to meet at his apartment for a takeout dinner. I went really crazy and bought a bunch of really gross tacos with lots of extra beans and cheese and hot sauce.

Sam seemed kind of distracted when I got there. I cracked a joke here and there, but he didn't even seem to notice.

"You okay?" I asked as I arranged the food on plates.

He shrugged. "Something weird happened today. Some stuff was ripped off from one of my job sites."

"Oh, no." I handed him a tub of hot sauce. He just put it on the table.

"Couple of bottles of pretty expensive liquor," he went on. "The people who own the house are really ticked off."

"Wow." I knew that a theft—even a small one—could ruin a contractor's reputation. "Which job?" I asked.

He frowned and looked down at his plate. "I'm not saying Bailey did it," he said.

"Wait a minute." Things were going way too fast. "You're saying it was the job Bailey was working on?"

Sam nodded. But he didn't look at me.

This was getting weird. "Of course he didn't do it," I said. The idea of Bailey stealing something—it was inconceivable. "Why would you even—"

"I know," he said, putting up his hands. He opened his mouth. Then he stopped again.

The silence between us was excruciating, and I knew there was more.

At last Sam said, "The thing is, I called Pete, the other guy who was working with him. And I asked him point-blank."

I nodded, sort of speechless, but needing to know.

Sam sighed heavily. "Pete said he worked outside the whole time. Couldn't go in because his boots were so muddy. So . . . I don't know what to think."

I shook my head. It couldn't be true. Not Bailey.

"You tell me," Sam said softly. "Is it possible?"

I was still shaking my head as my mind replayed the past few weeks with Bailey.

But I was already thinking, maybe it is possible after all.

God, it had probably been going on for longer . . . weeks, maybe months. Why hadn't I seen it earlier?

All the signs. The spaciness. The grouchiness. The frequent absences.

Yeah, Bailey had probably been the one who stole the liquor. When you've got his problem, you'll do anything for a drink.

I buried my face in my hands as the truth about Bailey rang in my head. My brother . . .

My brother, the drunk.

Chapter 11

You know how everyone talks about denial when
there's a drinking problem? Well, I clung to that
denial for a while after I first talked to Sam. In the
back of my mind I hoped that there was another
explanation for the missing liquor and for all of
Bailey's problems. I mean, I was on Bailey's side,
right?

But when I spilled the story to Sarah, she confirmed
my worst fears.

"He drinks all the time now," she said. "It's part of
the reason we broke up."

"Everybody drinks," I answered, trying to defend
my brother.

"Not like Bailey," Sarah said sadly. "He's like a
different person, Jule."

At last we decided to face Bailey together. We went
to his apartment, hoping to talk to him.

But the whole thing backfired. He accused us of ganging up on him. In fact, he did everything but slam the door in my face. My own brother.

And the weirdest part was that Bailey was always the brother I got along with. I mean, one of the reasons that Charlie and I were so much at odds now was that Bailey hadn't been around. Bay had a way of keeping Charlie's control thing in check.

But now Bailey was off in his own world, this really self-destructive world. And he didn't seem to have a clue that he was hurting himself.

The last thing I needed right now was another problem—another part of my life coming unglued. I mean, wasn't it bad enough that I didn't know what I wanted to do after graduation and that Charlie was trying to order me around and that none of us were really getting along at home?

More pressure? I thought. Sure, just toss it on top of the heap.

Anyway, since Bailey had closed the door on me, I had to go to the last person I wanted to talk with.

Charlie.

He wasn't an easy person to catch up with these days. Between watching Owen, managing Salinger's, and spending time with Grace, he was almost never home. But I was determined.

The day that Bailey closed me out, I made a point of waiting up for Charlie. It was late when I finally heard him come up the stairs and duck into the bathroom.

He was brushing his teeth when I poked my head in. "Charlie, we have to talk."

He glared up at me, toothpaste on his lips. Not the

most encouraging reaction, but I pressed on. "Something bad's going on with Bay."

"Oh, yeah?" He wiped his face, not even bothering to look at me. "Exactly what would that be?"

His coldness shocked me. "What's with the attitude?"

"No, go ahead," he said, his voice dripping with condescension. "Tell me *all* about it."

"Excuse me?" I said. "Can't we talk anymore?"

"Oh, sure. *Now* you want to talk. After you blow out of here and hide at Sam's—after all your crap, why should I talk to you at all?"

"This isn't about me. It's about Bailey."

"And how he's partying too much," he jumped in, stealing the words from me.

I reeled back. "You *know* about it? You know about it and you're not doing anything?"

"Bailey is fine," he said. "You just can't stand to see him enjoying himself, can you? You just want everyone else to be as . . . as miserable as you are!"

I stepped back, stunned. Charlie was being totally unfair, totally blind. And to blame it all on me . . . to believe that I was so selfish . . .

"You're wrong about this, Charlie," I said quietly. "Totally wrong."

"Let me give you a news flash here," he said, his eyes cold and cutting. "You're not the smartest person in the world, Jule. You don't know everything."

"Neither do you," I said. I pounded up the attic stairs to my room.

That's the last time I'll count on Charlie for anything, I vowed.

* * *

So everything had kind of hit this low point when the day of Owen's party arrived. Our family seemed to be melting down. But when the big day arrived, we all sort of sucked it up and put on our happy faces.

Charlie came through with some huge wrapped packages—probably toys of monster proportions. Colorful helium balloons and streamers bobbed and waved in the backyard. Claudia had gone a little overboard on the decorations, but Owen shrieked with delight when he saw the yard. And the cake was a huge hit, too.

"See?" Owen said after he'd lured a few kids into the kitchen to see the orange and blue Gummi animals. "You can eat them!"

"Just the ones on the side," I reminded him. The last thing we needed was for one of the kids to bite into the plastic Kooroo the Kangaroo from the top of the cake.

"Yeah," Owen said, pushing his birthday crown back on his head. "And I get *all* the blue ones."

"We'll see about that," I said. I hustled the kids out to the backyard, where Claudia was helping them into a huge moonwalk that we'd rented.

Standing in the doorway, I folded my arms and congratulated myself for a second. We'd pulled it off! Okay, Bailey and the clown were running late. But the yard looked great, the place was packed with happy kids, and the party was in full swing!

Owen let out a big laugh as he raced two of his friends over to the moonwalk, and I had to smile. Even Grace's parents, Rose and Martin Wilcox, who had shown up to help out, seemed to be having a good time, enjoying the kids. I had just met them that day, but they seemed a lot more genuine than their daughter. She wasn't winning any awards with the Salinger clan.

I went outside to join them. Grace's father was doing a magic trick for some of the kids. And Sam was standing there with Rose, talking a mile a minute, which is strange for him. He looked a little nervous, but I just assumed it was because he wasn't used to being around so many kids.

"Here," Sam said, pulling over a chair for Rose. "You have a seat and I'll refill your drink."

"Oh, you'll spoil me," Rose said, handing him her cup. Sam winked at me as he made his way to the party table, and Grace's mother smiled and said, "He's a nice boy."

I smiled back. Yeah, he was nice. And gorgeous.

If I could only figure out what was missing between us . . .

But I didn't have time to think about that now. Owen's friend Kerry ran up to me and held out her foot. "Tie my shoe, please," she piped out.

I knelt and made a bow in her sneaker. Then I stood and surveyed the yard. Things were really swimming along. Now, if the clown would just get here and wow the kids, it would be the perfect party.

Sam came back with the drinks. He was just handing me a glass of ginger ale, when his beeper went off.

"Oops! That'll be the site. I'd love to stay and talk, but I'd better get going," he said politely to Rose.

"That's okay," Grace's mother told him. "It's just part of having your own business."

"I'll say!" Sam nodded at her. "Nice meeting you."

I followed him into the house to say good-bye. He

paused in the foyer and flashed me a proud smile. "Did you see that?"

"See what?" I asked.

"You didn't notice? I was a saint to those people. I brought them drinks. Chatted with them. They've probably never been treated that good."

I stood there, frozen. *Those people?* God. Not again.

Sam didn't even pick up on my horror as he leaned down and kissed my cheek. "I'll try and swing by after work."

That was when I knew it would never work.

"Don't bother," I said slowly.

Already on his way out the door, Sam turned back and blinked. "Whoa. What's wrong? Did I do something?"

"Yeah," I said. "You did. And I know you probably don't think so. You probably think it was just . . . another joke. But I can't be with someone who thinks that way. Who can't deal with someone whose skin is a different color."

"That's what this is about? Didn't you see how I treated them?" He pointed out toward the yard. "I was a prince."

I shook my head. "But it's an issue with you. And when I think about the things you've said . . . the jokes you've made . . . I feel sick."

"So what, are you ending this?" He frowned as if I were being totally ridiculous. "That's insane. To just casually end a relationship over—"

"This isn't casual, Sam." He wasn't getting it, and the more he fought it, the worse I began to feel. "And it's been sort of in the air for a while. I mean, when we first got together, remember how we talked about falling in love? How sometimes it takes time to develop?"

"Sure." He folded his arms. "What, did we reach some invisible time limit or something?"

I shook my head. "No, it's not that. It's . . . it's a lot of things."

"Like what?" he said petulantly. "Politics? Race? Or are we back to the age thing?"

Tears stung my eyes and my throat got really tight. "If you knew how much I wanted this . . ."

God, why was this so hard?

"Look," he said, taking my hand. "This is stupid. It's a dumb argument about something that doesn't matter."

"Dumb?" I yanked my hand away. "I just spent five minutes telling you I care about this. Don't call it nothing." I swiped at the tears on my cheeks and took a deep breath.

"You'd better go," I told him.

He frowned. For a minute I thought he was going to keep arguing.

Then, at last, he turned and went out the front door. Sam was gone.

Chapter 12

Tears swam in my eyes as I crossed my arms and hurried through the house.

What am I crying about? I asked myself. I wasn't in love with Sam. I knew this relationship wasn't perfect.

But that wasn't it. I wasn't crying over Sam. I was crying because something I had hoped might turn into something great didn't. It just collapsed.

And I was crying because now there was one less certain thing in my life. One less thing to count on.

I took a deep breath. No way could I join the party like this. Everyone would think I was a total weirdo.

But I didn't have much choice, it seemed.

"Cake time!" Claudia called from the kitchen.

I watched as she lifted the lit cake.

"Give me that!" the clown said, snatching the cake away.

The clown! Finally, he'd arrived. An hour late, and equipped with major attitude.

Wait, I thought as I took a second look. I gasped.

It was Bailey! Bailey in a clown suit.

Oh, no. He'd messed up, I realized. Somehow, he'd totally botched his only job for the party.

He'd better put on a good show, I thought, standing back as he staggered out the back door, the tiny candle flames wavering in the breeze. Claudia followed him out, leading the song.

"Happy birthday to you! Happy birthday to you!" everyone sang.

I stood in the doorway, watching. Owen sat at the head of the table, beaming, as the clown held the cake in front of him.

"Now make a wish and blow out the candles," Claudia said.

Owen's cheeks puffed up with air, then he blew.

"Well," Bailey said, "that pretty much sucked."

"Bailey!" I called from the house. He was acting like a total jerk.

A wobbly jerk. As he lifted the cake and moved away from Owen, he stumbled on something and fell into two of the kids. Frosting smeared onto their shirts, and they screamed. Bailey veered away, trying to balance the cake.

"Oh, God!" My heart lurched as the kids began to whine and scream. Bailey swayed again, and Owen sank back in his chair with a frightened look.

"What's going on?" Claudia yelped.

"He's ripped," Charlie said in disbelief.

It was true. Bailey was drunk—totally wasted.

He wavered like a rag doll ready to fall over. Reaching up, he yanked off his hat and nose, scaring

Mitchell, a kid from down the block who stood near him.

"Okay," Bailey muttered. "S'okay. Just a little messed up."

But Mitchell wasn't buying it. Instead, his chin began to quiver as he stared up in horror. No wonder. Bailey was a scary sight, with his smeared clown makeup and his unfocused stare.

"Oh, come *on,*" Bailey yelled at him. "Don't cry. He's *crying.*"

"Come on, Bay," Charlie said, taking him by the arm. "Let's get out of here."

"I'm talking here." Bailey shook Charlie's arm off.

Charlie lunged at him for a better grip, then Bailey shoved him away . . . and suddenly my brothers were wrestling in the backyard. In the middle of Owen's party.

Before it was over, Bailey flung Charlie back into the swing. Charlie crashed to the ground, dazed and hurt.

Everyone got quiet. Even the kids were too amazed to react. All eyes turned to Bailey.

"He pushed—it was an accident," Bailey mumbled.

It was a totally lame excuse. But then again, what could he say? He was drunk and everyone knew it. Everyone except the kids. They were just scared and a little amazed.

Bailey glared at us, then turned and stumbled into the house. Claudia ran after him. That left Charlie and me to pick up the pieces and try to console a dozen little kids.

"So—who wants cake?" Charlie called.

I brought out paper towels and tried to wipe down

the kids who'd been smeared with frosting. But I kept checking the door, wondering what was going on inside.

What next? I thought. The day had started out so well.

Then suddenly, I'd lost my boyfriend. And my brother. And Owen's birthday party had disintegrated into a total nightmare.

The way I looked at it, things couldn't get much worse. I mean, my family was sinking into this black hole.

And I was getting dragged in right along with everyone else.

After the kids left, I headed outside and tried to wade through the mess in the backyard. Bailey had passed out inside. Claudia had disappeared. Charlie was helping Owen unwrap gifts.

The whole day was such a bust. And I couldn't bear this huge weight of worry about Bailey. Suddenly it all just crept up on me, and I found myself crying as I stuffed sticky plates and spoons into a trash bag. It was dark and I was alone, so it really didn't matter. I let the tears roll down my cheeks.

I was scraping frosting off the seat of the swing, when I heard a noise at the gate. It was Sarah.

"Hey!" She held out a gift. "This is for Owen. I figured I'd stop by when Bailey wasn't here and—" She paused. "Are you crying, Julia? What's wrong? What happened?"

"Everything." I sucked in a deep breath. "It's just so—screwed up." I told her what had happened with Bailey.

"Oh, my God," she said. "He was drunk, wasn't he?"

"Totally," I said. "He's passed out in Owen's room. We'll have to put Owen in with Claudia for the night." I sighed. "I guess Charlie finally . . . he finally sees it. But it's weird. I mean, it's one time when I wish I *wasn't* right."

She reached out and touched my arm. "Let's go inside."

The house was quiet and kind of eerie. Charlie and Grace were sitting in the living room. I could hear their conversation from the hall. They were arguing about—who else?—Bailey.

"He's in college, Grace. He's got crappy judgment. All that stuff. But he's not a—" Charlie paused, then blurted out, "He's exactly like I was then."

"Oh, really? Did you ever hit anyone in your family?" Grace asked him. "Because he hit you, Charlie."

"Look," Charlie said defensively. "I've been out of control just like that. He's just doing what I did."

"No, Charlie." I stepped into the room, into the shadowed light. "He's different."

Charlie and Grace swung toward me and Sarah, annoyed that we were butting in.

"You drank," I told my brother. "But you were always *you*. Bailey is . . . it's like he's disappearing. Like the person I grew up with is gone. When he drinks, he's just not Bay."

"She's right," Sarah said. "And Bailey is *so* far from facing it. I mean, he would never talk about it with me."

"You've got to deal with it, Charlie," Grace said

firmly. "If you keep denying it, you're just helping Bailey dig in deeper. You've got to face the problem. Talk about it. And confront Bailey."

I leaned against the back of the overstuffed chair. For once, I agreed with Grace.

Huh. First time for everything.

"So . . ." Charlie slumped over, staring at the floor. "So . . ." He drew in a breath and looked up, tears sparkling in his eyes. I could see that he was getting it. Really getting it.

I sank down into the big chair, feeling a strange flicker of warmth as we talked. After months of being at odds with Charlie, we were on the same side again. And Charlie was a good friend to have. Yes, he could drive you crazy with his stubbornness. But he had a good heart. And he was fiercely loyal.

Grace talked about this thing called intervention. She described it as a way to confront Bailey—all of us together—so that we could present a united front. So that we could all tell him we knew he had a problem, and that we were there for him.

"I think we should do it," I told Charlie.

He stared at the floor for a moment. Finally, he nodded.

"I'll be there," Sarah promised. "Just tell me where and when." She reached for her sweater. "It's late. Want to see if he's up? Maybe he'll let me give him a ride home."

I followed her up to Owen's room, where Bailey was sleeping it off. She opened the door slowly and I stood back as the light from the hallway cut through the darkness. It lit the bed, hit the rumpled bedcovers. I blinked.

The bed was empty.

"He must have woken up," Sarah said.

Biting back a feeling of alarm, I pushed past her into the room and rushed to the window. Outside, in the dark driveway . . .

"His Jeep is gone," I gasped. "He's gone."

"He's *driving?*" Sarah winced. "Oh, my God."

I nodded. Bailey was out there. Alone. And out of control.

Panic rose inside me like a huge wave. Way to go, Bay, I wanted to scream. Go out and get yourself killed.

It'll be one birthday we'll never forget.

Chapter 13

I don't think any of us slept that night. Charlie kept calling Bailey's new girlfriend, Callie, even though she promised to call the minute he showed up. The din of the television rumbled on as Charlie paced in the living room.

I went up to the attic and played some music, waiting, checking the window. And waiting. Downstairs I heard Claudia playing her violin at three in the morning. It was really crazy.

Finally, at six, I called Callie. She told me that Bailey had come back. Only she was asleep when he came in, so she hadn't called.

Can you believe it? I mean, we were *frantic,* and she knew Bay was okay but didn't call. I guess Callie is one of those people who's totally wrapped up in her own world. And meanwhile, my brother Bailey was hitting bottom.

We had to help him. And we had to do it now—
before it was too late.

So we tried this big intervention thing yesterday, I
wrote to Griffin one night. *It was . . .*

I stopped writing and lay there on my bed. Tears
welled up in my eyes as I remembered.

It was the worst day of my life.

Even worse, in a way, than when we got the news
about our parents. Then, there was shock . . .
horror . . . pain. But with Bay . . .

*It was almost like watching him die while he was
still standing right there in front of us,* I wrote. *I mean,
what happened to the old Bailey? My brother? Instead,
there was this stranger in our living room who looked
just like him, but who wasn't him. At all. He was nasty,
and hard, and cruel.*

I rolled over and sat back against the pillows, biting
the end of my pen. Going back over those horrible
hours.

It had been wrong from the start. First of all, we
couldn't get Bailey to meet us. I mean, he kept
agreeing to have a family dinner at Salinger's, but
then not showing up. Obviously, he was avoiding us.

Finally, we decided we had to trick him into
coming over. So we talked Claudia into calling him
and pretending Owen was hurt.

It worked. But it was wrong. All wrong. It tore
Claudia apart to do it. And when Bailey got there, and
found out we used our little sister and our baby
brother to trick him. . . .

It felt horrible. Sickening. Like we were the ones
who were hurting Bay, instead of the other way
around.

And then—then, when we tried to tell him that he had a problem, he . . . attacked.

I started writing again. *Oh, God, Griffin, he said the most horrible things. He ripped us apart—each of us, one by one. He went down the line, took our deepest, most painful secrets and twisted them into these ugly . . .*

A tear ran down my cheek, then another and another. They splashed onto the letter, smearing the black ink.

But it wasn't even the things he said, I wrote. *I mean, yeah, they hurt. A lot. But the really horrible part was the fact that he was saying them at all. I mean, Bailey. Sweet, kind Bailey.*

I'm not sure he exists anymore.

And it's not just Bailey that's vanishing. I haven't even gotten to the final nightmare. I haven't told you about what happened when Dad's old partner, Joe, stopped by. Charlie thought maybe Joe could help with Bailey.

Some help. Do you know what he told us?

I stared up at the ceiling. Thinking about this part made me feel numb. Frozen inside.

Joe said that our father—*our father*—was an alcoholic, too. That the reason we never saw him take a drink was that he quit when Bailey was born. Because he knew that he could never stop at just one.

At first I'd wanted to scream that Joe was a liar. That he was making all this stuff up for some twisted reason of his own.

But I could see in his eyes that he was telling the truth. And then Charlie confirmed it, remembering the way Mom and Dad used to fight, and Dad used to come home so late some nights. . . .

92

So it was true. The dad we all thought we knew wasn't real. Our real father was a drunk.

And Bailey was just following in his footsteps.

My pen moved over the paper. *What is happening to my family? Does it even exist anymore? Did it ever exist?*

I feel like I've just been cut loose. I'm drifting. Just a little while ago I had a life. I had a family. A history. Things I was sure of. I had all these plans.

But now I have nothing.

Downstairs, I heard Owen call my name. "Joo-yah! Joo-yah!"

I'd just put him to bed for, like, the sixth time. Claudia, Charlie, and I were doing our best to cover, but the truth—which none of us wanted to actually say—was that Owen missed Bailey.

I sighed. Maybe he would go back to sleep.

I don't want to be selfish. I don't want to make it sound as if this is about me. But I'm so scared, Griffin. I feel like this is destroying us all. Like we're all sealed in these little pods of pain. We hurt so much we can't help each other.

It's so lonely.

God, I wish you were here.

"Joo-yah!" Owen cried again. He shouted out a string of unintelligible words, then burst into tears.

I tossed down my pen and climbed off the bed to go console my little brother.

I ran down the attic stairs and automatically turned toward Owen's room. Halfway down the hall I nearly collided with Charlie, who had the sleepy-eyed, mussed-hair look of someone who'd just rolled out of bed.

"Thanks, Jule," he snapped. "He's only been calling you for, like, twenty minutes."

"Go back to bed, Charlie," I said evenly.

"Who can sleep with him crying?" He rubbed his eyes. "God, it's just constant around here."

"He's three years old," I said, pushing past him. "Anyway, I don't remember volunteering to be night nurse." Marching into Owen's room, I switched on the light—and stopped in my tracks.

Claudia was there, sitting on the edge of his bed, rubbing his back. "It's okay, buddy," she said, leaning close to him. She shielded her eyes against the light and added, "Would you shut that thing off?"

I switched it off and waited in the doorway while she kissed him, tucked the covers under his chin, and tiptoed out.

"Let's hope he's out for the night," I said.

Claudia shrugged, then stared up at me with big, hollow eyes. "What are you and Charlie fighting about now?"

"Nothing. I don't know. We're all so freaked out about Bailey. It's like he's everything now and we're . . . we're just in the background."

Suddenly Claudia's eyes filled with tears.

"What is it?"

"It's just . . . our whole family is falling apart. And I don't know how to fix it. I don't know what to do."

"I know what you mean," I said. I touched her shoulder, but she turned away and went back to her room. "I wish *I* could fix things," I said under my breath. "I really do."

During those days I was glad that I still had to finish my senior year at school. Sure, I was bored with the assignments and stuff. But it helped to have somewhere to go where everybody wasn't moping around.

I was sitting in my last class, when Justin slid a library book in front of me. It was a copy of *The Sun Also Rises* by Ernest Hemingway.

"You starting a new colony of the Lost Generation?" I asked.

"Charter member," he said, pointing at himself. "I just reread that. Paris is back on the list." He was talking about the list of places he planned to see when he backpacked through Europe this summer.

"Paris was always on the list, you idiot," I told him. This was an ongoing conversation—sort of a game we played at least once a week, "where to go in Europe." Of course, avoiding the major tourist traps without cutting out the total classic cities like Paris and Florence.

"You've always been a sucker for Paris, Jules."

I smiled. Then the bell rang. Justin scooped up the book. Saying something about meeting his girlfriend, Robyn, he disappeared in the shuffle.

I envied him. His life seemed so on track. So sane. I mean, he had a plan that he liked, and he was excited about the future. Why couldn't my life be that way, too?

Outside in the hall I stacked books in my locker and slammed the door. Sarah caught up to me to ask about the English assignment.

"It's one of those index card things," I explained. Our English teacher had adopted this weird system to keep book reports short. They had to fit on a five-by-seven index card.

"It's supposed to be one paragraph of summary, one paragraph of critique. All on one side of the card.

Typed or handwritten. And if it doesn't fit on the card, Allender won't read it."

"Due Monday?" Sarah asked. When I nodded, she pushed open the red fire door and groaned. "The man has no mercy."

I followed her in the usual after-school daze. You know how you walk along out of focus, ignoring the blur of faces and trees and buses outside the school.

Then something struck me as out of place. I turned back to take a second look.

There, on the steps, leaning against the brick wall of the school . . .

Oh, God.

My heart seemed to swell until I thought it would burst.

It couldn't be. It was impossible.

But it was real. *He* was real.

Griffin.

Chapter 14

"Oh, my God." I walked right over and let out an incredulous laugh. "You're back!"

His hazel eyes sparked as he studied me, almost as if he couldn't believe he was really seeing me again. But all he said was "Uh-huh."

Well, Griffin never was a big talker.

"What are you doing here? When did you get back? How did you know I was here?" The questions tumbled out of my mouth.

He just smiled and spread his arms a little. An invitation? I wasn't sure. But I couldn't let the chance slip away.

"Griffin." I fell against him and hugged him. He seemed stiff for a minute, then he hugged me back, and it felt so good, so right, that I didn't want to let go.

"Wow. Did you get my letters?" I asked.

"Yeah. I guess so. I don't know. Most of 'em, I

think. Unless you sent any in the last couple of weeks." He shifted his weight slightly. "You want to . . . go somewhere?"

"Sure," I said. I tried to sound casual. But the truth was, from the minute I saw Griffin I was sort of knocked over by this wave of feeling. I didn't want to let him go. Literally. It took a major effort to pry my fingers off the sleeve of his leather jacket so that we could get into the car.

We ended up at the Coffee House, where we plunked down on the sofa we always used to sit on and ordered the coffees we always used to drink. Everything had that velvety feeling of something old and familiar, like your favorite T-shirt after you've washed it a million times.

It just happened so naturally. Griffin asked me one or two questions, and suddenly the words were spilling out in a breathless rush. I told him everything. About Bailey. About Owen's party. About the intervention.

". . . and last night Claudia slept in the living room because she was afraid she'd miss the phone ringing," I told him. "You know—in case Bailey called to say 'I made a mistake, I want to quit drinking, take me back.'"

Griffin just shook his head. But I could tell that he got it, that he totally understood, without saying a word.

"And yesterday? Yesterday I was driving home, kind of in Bailey's neighborhood. So I decided to swing by and see if his car was there—which it wasn't. But guess whose was? Charlie's. He was sitting there, same as me, hoping to see Bailey."

Griffin nodded again. His hazel eyes were full of

sympathy. It was almost as if he were saying to me, I know, I understand exactly how you feel. He didn't say a word, but that's the message he got across. That's the thing that happens when Griffin and I are together. Total connection.

"Order's up," the counter guy called.

We got up and went to the counter to pick up our coffee. Griffin was a step behind me, and suddenly I realized he'd lagged behind when we'd walked in from the car.

"Hey." I checked out his well-worn jeans. "Are you limping?"

"No. Not really. My leg gets stiff when I'm off it for a while. So—what about Bailey's new girl, Callie?" he asked as we went back to our sofa. Obviously, he was trying to change the subject. "Does she say anything?"

I refused to back off. "Griffin, you *are*. You're limping."

"It's no big deal. I just—I fell on the boat."

"You *fell*? When was this?" I prodded.

He shrugged. "A few months ago."

Months ago? "And you're still limping?" A horrible feeling came over me as the whole picture took shape. Griffin had been hurt. And if the injury hadn't healed by now, it must have been really serious.

"It's just some scar tissue in the knee joint," Griffin said, tossing it off with a shrug. "It's no biggie. The doctor says I'll be back to normal in a few months."

"But . . ." I stared at him for a minute, kind of shocked that he hadn't mentioned this. "I just . . . I can't believe you didn't write about it. Or call or something. I mean, you must have been in a lot of pain, with time on your hands and everything."

"Yeah. They gave me stuff for the pain, and it all got

to be a blur after a while. I mean, I couldn't work anymore. But it was totally their fault, so no one expected me to work."

"Really?" I licked a dab of foam from the rim of my cup. "How'd it happen?"

"They sent me up this bulkhead without a bosun's rating."

It was all Greek to me. I squinted at him. "In English?"

"I . . . well, it wasn't really my job. Totally against union rules. And that's how I got hurt."

"Right. So it seems to me that they owe you something."

He laughed. "Probably seems a little different to them."

"Well, sure. But maybe you should sue."

"Sue?" Now he looked at me as if *I* were speaking Greek. "Like, go to court?"

I nodded. "It's a good idea, Griffin. Really. I could help you get a lawyer. And maybe they could get you whatever money they owe you and then . . . then you could buy yourself some time."

He still looked puzzled. "Time? For what?" He shook his head. "No, no, I'm not into that stuff. Lawsuits." His face screwed up as if he'd just gotten a taste of something bitter.

"Griffin . . ." I swallowed back a sigh, feeling a familiar flicker of frustration. He could travel all over the world, and still come back kind of clueless.

"Griffin, it's *their* fault. Because of them you got hurt. They owe you a chance to get your life together. A chance to take a break before you get another job. A change to do something fun, like go traveling. With a friend . . ."

Something flashed in his eyes. "A friend?" He studied me, searching . . . almost getting it.

"I want to get out of here," I said, spelling it out. "Don't you?"

"I just *got* here," he said. But he didn't sound certain.

I pulled my knees onto the couch and turned toward him. "I want to go someplace great with you. I want you to take me away someplace great."

"Really?" He seemed surprised. As if he'd never considered that possibility. As if I'd just suggested this outlandish thing.

I shook my head. "Sometimes I just don't get what's going on in your head," I said. "Like all this. I mean, this is major. Why didn't you say anything?"

"I don't know." He took a sip of coffee, then stared at the wall as if the answer were printed there but it was difficult to decipher. "I guess . . . I guess I was afraid you'd be disappointed."

"Disappointed?" I couldn't believe what I was hearing. "Because you hurt your knee?"

"No . . ." He was still staring at the wall. "Because . . . see, the doctor doesn't want me on the boat. So that kind of means I'm out of a job."

I tossed a strand of hair out of my eyes. "So?"

"So . . . I didn't have a chance to do everything I wanted. I really wanted to come home with all that stuff you said. You know . . . like a job and—and a *purpose.*"

A purpose. I thought about the heavy conversation we'd had just before Griffin had left. His heart was definitely in the right place, but his head . . . He just didn't see the opportunity that was about to jump up and bite him.

"All that stuff we talked about," I said. "It's not—things change."

He gave me this "Oh, come on!" look. "Last time I talked to you, you had a twenty-year plan going."

"Yeah, well . . ." I sat back and smoothed my sweater out. "Lately I haven't been planning so far in advance."

"Oh." He smiled. "Like you know how many kids you're going to have, but you haven't named them yet?"

"Nothing like that," I insisted, looking him in the eyes. It was so good having him back. I reached out and touched his hand, and those amazing sparks shot through me.

"In fact, right now . . . right now I'd be happy if I could just plan on spending some time with you."

Chapter 15

When I got home that night it was sort of like washing ashore on this incredible wave. Suddenly, my life wasn't falling apart anymore. Griffin was back. We could be together again. And he would help me keep my head above water.

I felt light-headed as I tossed my coat on the bench. Then I glanced into the kitchen and saw them— Charlie and Claudia and Sarah—looking really stressed.

The old heaviness crashed back down on me. "What happened?" I demanded. "Did Bailey call?"

"Bay picked Owen up from day care without telling anybody," Charlie explained. "They're not back yet."

"What do you mean?" I searched their faces, trying to get the whole story. Why was that such a big deal? "Where are they?"

"We don't know," Sarah answered quietly.

"And it's been hours," Claudia said tensely. "He picked Owen up *four hours* ago."

"Oh, my God!" I pressed a hand to my mouth. If Bailey was driving around drunk with Owen . . .

There was nothing we could do. Nothing but wait. Charlie had already called the day care center a zillion times. He'd called all the hospitals. Finally, he even called the police. But no one had any answers for us.

It was excruciating. When you're waiting like that, you have time to think of the terrible things that can happen. Like when your parents go out and never come home because they were killed by a drunk driver. I mean, it takes only one horrible minute. And suddenly your life has been smashed up and nothing is the same.

Where *was* Bailey?

Were we going to get the call that *he'd* been in an accident? That *he'd* killed someone's parents?

I don't know how long we waited. But it was dark outside when I heard the Jeep pull in. I bolted out to find Bailey strolling into the backyard with Owen.

"What the hell do you think you're doing?" I yelled at Bailey. I snatched my baby brother into my arms and hugged him close. "Are you okay, Owe?" Then I held him away from me, taking inventory. "Let me look at you."

"Of course he's okay," Bailey growled.

"Bailey's my favorite brother," Owen announced.

"Well, that makes one of you," I muttered as Charlie and the others ran out into the yard. I whisked Owen toward the door, hoping to shield him from the inevitable fireworks.

I was too late.

"Where the *hell* have you been?" Charlie ripped into Bailey. "Where the *hell* have you been?"

"I took Owen for a ride," Bailey yelled back. "Why the *hell* does that matter?"

That pushed Charlie over the edge. He pointed at Bailey, getting right in his face. "You picked him up without telling anyone? And then you kept him all day without calling?"

I held Owen just inside the doorway, afraid to let him see his brothers. Even more afraid of what might happen if I disappeared inside.

"I spent the afternoon with my little brother," Bailey said, his voice booming with bravado. "I do it all the time."

"No, you don't," Charlie spat out. "The last few weeks you've been totally AWOL."

"So I'm making up for lost time," Bailey argued.

"No!" Charlie growled. "I won't have you taking him, driving around . . . and we don't know if . . ."

"If I'm *wasted?*" Bailey snarled. "Is that what this is about?"

I pressed Owen's head onto my shoulder. All I could hope was that he didn't understand.

"Well? Are you? Are you?" Charlie demanded. "Let me smell your breath." He took a step toward Bailey.

"Get away from me," Bay growled, ducking away.

"You are!" Charlie accused, his face tight with fury. "You've been drinking."

"One beer!" Bailey insisted.

I shook my head. How could he? How *could* he?

Charlie threw his arms wide. "You drank and you drove with our little brother in the car?"

"I'm totally sober," Bailey insisted.

But Charlie wasn't backing off. He lunged toward Bay with a rage that really scared me.

"I can't believe you!" Charlie shouted, shoving Bailey.

Bailey raised his fists and shoved Charlie right back.

"I can't *believe* you!" Charlie pounded him again.

This time Bailey's reaction resembled a punch.

"Stop it!" Claudia cried. "Stop it! Julia!" She turned to me, tears shining in her eyes.

I plunked Owen down on the floor and rushed outside. "No, Charlie! Don't!" I wrapped my arms around him, pulling him away from Bailey. I could feel him shaking in my arms, trembling with rage as we shuffled backward.

"Stay away from Owen!" Charlie shouted at Bailey.

"He's my brother," Bailey snarled.

But Charlie was swinging his head from side to side furiously, trying to shake me off. "No he's not! Not anymore!"

Bailey shot a look at all of us. Then his face crumpled.

"You people . . ." he began. Tears glistened in his eyes.

Then he turned and cut out. Just cut out, like he didn't even care about working things out.

Working things out?

Impossible, I told myself as I helped Claudia get Owen ready for bed. Claudia had been right the other night. Our family was falling apart. Crumbling.

And there was nothing I could do to fix it. I felt powerless . . . exhausted.

I needed to get away.

I needed Griffin.

It was hard to drive. Talk about out of control. Once I had to pull to the side of the road and double over till the sobbing stopped. Tears kept filling my eyes, but I brushed them away and held tight to the steering wheel.

At last, the fluorescent hotel sign swam before my eyes. I pulled the car into a parking spot and tried to pull myself together as I stepped out into the cold air. I was almost there. I just had to find Griffin's room.

"Hey," he said when he opened the door. He put aside a cardboard bowl of cereal. Probably his dinner. "If I'd known you were coming, I would have fixed the good cereal." He cracked a smile.

I stood there, trying not to break down. But it was useless. My hands flew to my face as I burst into tears once more.

"Hey, whoa," he said softly. "Is it Bailey?"

I nodded. I wanted to explain, but I couldn't stop crying.

There was a minute while nothing happened. I think Griffin was trying to figure out what on earth was going on. Then he pulled me into his arms and let me cry against his chest.

"You're okay," he said, patting my back gently. "You're going to be okay. I'm right here."

For a while we just stood there. I cried. He held me.

When I finally had a chance to catch my breath, I pulled back to look at him. His eyes were so soft as he gazed down at me.

I leaned up and kissed him, and it felt so . . . right.

I ran my hands over his shirt, feeling his strength, his warmth. I started pulling on the buttons. Then we tumbled back onto the bed. Griffin's lips found mine again in a deep, yearning kiss.

It totally took my breath away.

My pulse was hammering in my ears when he pulled back with a tender, almost frightened look in his eyes. We both knew where this was going.

"Are you sure?" he whispered.

I knew what he was afraid of. He was scared that I was just falling into his arms in a weak moment.

He was wrong.

He cradled my face in one hand and repeated. "Are you sure . . . that this is right?"

For once, it was an easy question. I nodded, then kissed him again.

With a hungry sound he kissed me back and pulled me against him. It felt good and bittersweet and exciting.

"I'm sure," I whispered against his lips. "It's the only thing I *am* sure of."

Chapter 16

Slivers of sunlight cut through the blinds and played across the floor of the hotel room. I rolled over and cupped my hands over the muscles in Griffin's shoulders. "Good morning."

"Is it?" He turned toward me and punched the pillow under his head. His eyes held a question. "I was afraid one of us was going to suddenly wake up and decide that last night was a mistake. Like, say, you."

I sat up. Leaning against the headboard, I closed my eyes to think that one over. A mistake? No, last night had been the only right thing I'd done lately.

Of course, I knew Charlie would be on my case about being out all night. But he'd get over it.

"No," I told Griffin. "It wasn't a mistake. Because now we're, like, really *together*. And I want that. Don't you?"

"Yeah," he said.

I pulled the sheet up to my shoulders and hugged my knees to my chest. "It's kind of weird," I said. "But when I first saw you—and when we were together, last night—it was just . . . it was what I need right now. It felt so great."

He yanked on my arm, and I slid down in the bed till my face was even with his. "That's good." He ran a finger along my chin. "This is good, right? I mean, us?" When I nodded, he smiled. "Good. Because I've got someone you should meet."

"Who?"

"You'll see."

"But who is it?" I persisted. "Someone from the ship? Or did one of your long-lost relatives suddenly surface?"

"It's a surprise, sort of." He threw off the covers and slid out of bed. "Better get dressed first," he added.

"Duh!" I laughed and threw a pillow at him.

When Griffin led me into the lobby of a small office building and paused to check the directory, I figured it out. "A lawyer!" I said, smiling. "You're going to do the lawsuit."

He shrugged. "Seems like it might work." He ran his finger down to the H's. "Arnie Horne. Fifth floor."

A few floors up, a receptionist directed us into a shabby office—worn gray carpeting, metal file cabinets, a few framed newspaper clippings on the wall, and a desk that looked as if it would collapse under the overstuffed files stacked on it.

Arnie Horne introduced himself with a handshake and an oily smile that made me wonder if he was running for office. From the moment we sat down, he started to work the room, pacing behind his desk as if he were addressing a jury.

I flashed Griffin a look that said: *Is this guy for real?* But he just folded his hands and tried to look ultraserious.

"I must admit, the facts of this case are very compelling, Kevin," Arnie Horne began.

"Griffin," I corrected him. "His name is Griffin."

"Right. But the truth is, you are David going up against a greedy corporate Godzilla. And to think you can fight the good fight without ever stooping to the level of your enemy—this is naive."

I found it hard to follow the string of mixed metaphors. "What are you saying exactly?" I asked.

Arnie leaned against his desk. "Only that liability law is very tricky. And when it comes to making a case, some facts are better than others."

"But Griffin is *actually* hurt," I pointed out. "And it's *actually* their fault. What other facts do you need?"

"I'm simply reminding you that justice is blind." He waved his hand in front of his face and pretended that he couldn't see it. "Which sometimes means she misses things."

Griffin leaned forward. "So make sure they see the limp?"

"Your boyfriend is very smart," Arnie told me, patting Griffin on the back.

Just then the phone rang and Arnie dashed to pick it up. "Easy there, Sal. No need to shout," he said into the phone. "Oh, yeah? Well, jail is good for some people. Teaches them that—" Just then he seemed to remember that Griffin and I were watching and listening in. "I'd better take this next door." He punched the hold button and went out the door.

"Oh, wow!" I laughed as soon as he disappeared. "This guy is amazing! Should we sneak out of here now, or would he sue us for that?"

"What are you talking about?" Griffin asked, shifting in his chair. "Don't you like Arnie?"

"You don't need a likable guy, Griffin. You need a *lawyer.*"

"He's won tons of cases," Griffin said defensively. "Didn't you see his clippings?"

"But what judge in his right mind is going to trust this guy?" I was starting to feel frustrated. Sometimes Griffin just didn't seem that in touch with the real world. "I feel like he's selling me a used car. I mean, how did you pick this loser?"

From the look in Griffin's eyes, you would've thought I'd called *him* a loser. Okay, maybe I was a little harsh. But I couldn't just sit here and let him do something majorly stupid again—like hiring this sleazy attorney.

"I'm sorry you feel that way," he said with a tight voice. "I thought you'd be happy that I was going ahead with the suit."

"I am," I insisted. "It's just that this is serious. There's a lot of money involved. Don't let this guy blow it for you."

"You know, I really hate it when you do this," Griffin said, his voice rising. "It's the same deal every time. Give Griffin something to handle, but watch out—he'll screw it up. He always does."

"I'm not talking about *you,* Griffin. This is about him."

"No." He shook his head emphatically. "This is

about us. You second-guess everything I do. And . . . I mean, you have to trust me a little."

I reached over and touched his hand. "I do. I really do. But it's because I care that I push you. That's why we should get out of here. Now."

I stood up, ready to bolt. But Griffin sat back in the chair, holding his ground.

"I told Arnie I'd give him the case," he said quietly. "And I'm not going back on my word."

I stood there glaring as Arnie returned and started his spiel again. I was ticked off.

But then I began to think about it.

Maybe Griffin had a point. Maybe I did second-guess him. And if he was going to take control of his life, well, that meant I would have to stand back and stop trying to control him.

This is what you wanted, I reminded myself. For Griffin to take charge. Take control.

Still, it felt weird. It was hard to watch him do something that seemed so clearly wrong.

But as I stood there watching Griffin deal with Mr. Sleaze, I started to feel better about it. Griffin was changing. Growing up. Taking control.

And for the first time in what seemed like forever, I began to feel as if maybe everything was going to be okay.

That good feeling lasted until I got home. I had barely set foot into the kitchen, when Charlie was on my back.

"Where have you been?" he demanded. "You can't just disappear overnight like that, Julia."

I bristled at first. Then, when I saw the tired, almost hopeless look on his face, my stomach lurched.

"What's wrong?" I asked. "Charlie, what's—?"

"Bailey," he said quietly. "He had an accident."

"What?" I grabbed his arm.

"Last night. Sarah was in the car, and she got hurt—"

"Oh, my God." Suddenly I found it hard to breathe. Sort of like there was a weight pushing the air out of me.

This was what we'd all feared. What we'd been waiting for.

"She's in the hospital with a concussion. I mean, she's going to be okay, but—"

"Where's Bailey?" I asked. "Charlie, is he—"

"I don't know." The worry really showed on Charlie's face. From his red eyes and scruffy beard, I guessed he must have been up all night. "I mean, he got her there, so he must be okay. But then he disappeared."

"We've got to find him. He's probably sobered up by now." I put a hand on my brother's arm. "Charlie, it'll be okay."

Tears filled his eyes and he turned away from me. "It won't, Jule. It's not even close to okay. He could have gotten her killed. He could have killed Owen. I thought he would come around . . . that we were doing the right thing. I was wrong."

My throat felt tight and dry. What was Bailey doing to us?

"We'll find him," I said. "We'll make it okay, Charlie."

We spent the whole day and night searching for Bailey. Charlie called everyplace we could think of, and I drove around San Francisco, checking places where we used to hang out.

It was dark and I was really tired when I headed toward his apartment one more time. All day long I'd been going through stuff in my head, planning what I'd say to him when I found him. And as I searched the faces at the shadowed coffee house and turned away, I thought of a few more choice words for my brother.

I was totally annoyed. I wanted to be done with him.

But I couldn't bear the thought of losing him.

"Don't do something stupid, Bay," I said aloud as I watched the deserted door to his apartment. "Please don't be an idiot."

Chapter 17

It was after midnight when I collapsed on the living room couch. Charlie was there, waiting for the phone to ring, while some old TV show droned on. Claudia had crashed in a chair, too exhausted to go on, too scared to go to her own bed.

When we heard the noise at the back door, Charlie and I looked at each other. Claudia lurched up, suddenly awake, just as he came through the door.

"Bailey," she said, her voice hoarse from sleep.

"Where were you?" I demanded.

"Man, it gets worse with you every day," Charlie told him. "You were drunk, weren't you? Weren't you?"

Bailey blinked, a little stunned by our attacks, I think. Then, quietly, he answered, "Yes. But Sarah's okay."

"Like that makes it all right!" I shrieked.

"We didn't know what happened to you," Claudia said gently.

"Look," Bailey said, "I know. I know what it's like—"

"No. You don't," I interrupted. "You have no idea. You weren't here, going nuts every time the phone rang, thinking it was going to be some—some person with that *voice*, saying 'Is this the family of Bailey Salinger? Are you his next of kin?'"

Claudia turned her dark gaze up to him. "You can't keep doing this to us."

"I'm sorry," Bailey mumbled.

He looked so tired. So alone. But I couldn't soften to him now.

"That doesn't mean anything," I said.

"Where's this going?" Charlie demanded. "Are you going to keep drinking until you kill yourself? Is that the plan?"

"No," Bailey insisted. *"No.* I can't stand it anymore. I mean, there was blood. In the Jeep. There was her blood, I had it on me." His head dropped as if he were suddenly too weak to go on. "I'm done. It's over. I'm not going to drink. I'll go to meetings and . . . rehab . . . whatever."

I swallowed past the lump in my throat.

"I'm not sure I believe you," I said.

"I know." He pulled his wallet out of his back pocket, took out a thin card, and handed it to me. "Take this." I looked down at the card—his fake ID. "If I don't have it, I won't get into bars. I can't buy beers. Just get rid of it."

I went into the kitchen and pulled the shears out of the silverware drawer. Back in the living room I handed them to Bailey. "You do it."

We stood there, the three of us, watching in silence, as if it were some weird ritual or something. And as Bailey held up the scissors and sliced through the card, I made a wish for him.

I hope you mean this, Bay. I hope you mean it.

Within the next week, Bailey began to make good on his promise. He started going to Alcoholics Anonymous meetings. He called it quits with Callie. I guess the way she handled his drinking showed him what she was really like.

Finally, Bailey moved back home. It was a temporary thing—just so he could recoup and save some money for another place. We were tight on space again, but if it helped Bailey stay straight, I figured we'd survive.

Besides, I wasn't hanging at home much anymore. I spent every minute I could with Griffin, and it was great.

One afternoon when I showed up at his room, he was talking on the phone, so intent that he didn't even hang up when I got there. He just let me in with the phone to his ear. The whole thing didn't really hit me until he hung up and just stood there with a dazed look on his face.

"Griffin?" I said, a little scared. "Is something wrong?"

"That was Arnie Horne. The lawyer," he said. "The ship offered a settlement."

He looked numb, and I realized that he'd gotten some bad news on the phone. "You can go back to them, you know," I said quickly. "You don't have to accept the first offer. Or you could get another lawyer. You could—"

He shook his head. "It's a hundred. A hundred thousand. I get a hundred thousand. Dollars."

"Oh, my God." I gasped. "Oh. My *God!*" I leaped into the air as adrenaline shot through me. It was *great* news. The best!

Griffin smiled as the truth began to sink in. "I can move out of this rat hole. Get a decent place. And I won't have to take some crap job." He spun around and spread his arms wide. "And us! You! What do you want? You want a pony? A Porsche?"

I swung into his arms, and we both collapsed in laughter.

"This is wild!" I yelled. "It's insane!"

"Totally nuts. *Me.* When does stuff like this happen to *me?*"

"Today!"

"Yeah." Suddenly he got quiet. "And you know what? It's all because of you. You're the one who pushed me to do this. I mean, before we talked about it, I never even thought . . . it just never would've happened without you."

"So . . . maybe we're supposed to be together," I said.

"Maybe," Griffin answered with a slow smile.

Then he sat up. "So I have to stop by Arnie's to sign papers. Then there's the check to pick up and deposit. . . ."

As I sat back and watched him plan, I felt really happy. Finally, things were coming together. Bailey was on the wagon. Charlie and I were talking again. Griffin had a future now.

And because he wasn't tied down anymore, *I* suddenly had a future, too.

Not long ago I'd dreamed of spending the summer touring Europe on my own. But this was even better. To spend the summer seeing the world with Griffin . . . could anything be better?

It wasn't just a consolation prize.

This time I'd won the lottery.

Chapter 18

"Okay. Yell when you've found the spot," I told Griffin.

We were in the Coffee House, where I'd spread a map of North America over a table so that we could pick out a spot for spring break. It was sort of a game, like pin the tail on the donkey. Griffin had his eyes closed, and he was running his finger over the map in search of the magic spot.

"This is stupid," he muttered, his eyes still closed. "Why don't we just say we're going to Oregon or the Grand Canyon or something?"

"What fun is that? This has to be totally random. Like chance. Fate. The will of the gods. But keep your finger on the map," I said. "Otherwise we'll end up spending spring break in the crack of this table."

"Either that or I'll have coffee in my lap." He opened his eyes and frowned.

"No peeking!" I laughed. It felt incredibly good to have this whole block of time—all of spring break—stretched out before me. And the only plan was to spend that time with Griffin.

The best part was the potential. Sitting there with the map spread on the table, I felt excitement crackling in the air. This was my chance to go off and test my wings, explore, figure out where my life was going.

"Okay, okay," Griffin said with resolve. "Here we go. We're going to spend spring break in . . ." He stabbed his finger into the map and we both checked the spot.

"The Pacific Ocean?" he said.

I shook my head. "Not unless your bike doubles as a Jet Ski."

"You'd better try," Griffin told me. "It was your idea."

I closed my eyes, barely able to keep from laughing. "Watch and learn," I said, feeling like some mystic who was conjuring spirits. My finger hovered, swirling over the map. Then I jabbed it and checked the spot.

"Carson City, Nevada," I announced. "Let's hit the road."

"Cool."

We tossed back the last of our coffee and pushed away from the table. I slung my knapsack over my shoulder and turned toward the door.

"Hey, don't you want the map?" Griffin asked, reaching for it.

"Nope. So what if we get lost? That's kind of the point." I moved onto my toes to kiss him.

He grinned, tossed the map into the trash, and followed me out the door.

Flying.

That's how it felt riding on the back of Griffin's bike. The wind whipped around us and the sky was like a huge blue door above us, and it seemed so open and inviting. I felt as if we really had wings. It was as though the wheels of the motorcycle weren't touching the ground anymore.

I dug my fingers into Griffin's jacket and laughed aloud as we soared down a hill past a meadow full of grazing horses. I had sort of given up on ever feeling this way again. Totally free.

But now that Griffin was back, my entire life had changed. He got me away from the craziness at home. He was right beside me when I needed adventure, when I needed to break out. And he loved me.

It was sort of like the old Julia was outgrowing her shell, and Griffin was there to help me shed it.

That first day, as we sped down the highway and cruised through small towns, I had a lot of time to think. I thought about all the terrible things that I'd gone through—Libby's death and the fight over Stanford and Bailey's drinking and Sam and nearly getting squashed by Charlie's control thing.

I'd been through a lot, and I was still confused about where I was going. But now I wondered if all that painful stuff had a purpose. Sort of like it had to happen so that I could get here—with Griffin.

We were meant to be together. I knew that. And maybe I had needed a total life shake-up, maybe I'd needed to work through the college trap and all that family stuff so that I'd be free to take off with Griffin. To live for now and not for the future.

Griffin shifted to a lower gear when the sign appeared ahead of us: WELCOME TO NEVADA.

He pulled to the side of the road and rolled to a stop.

"Need a break?" I asked as I swung my leg over the bike and stretched my arms.

"Not that. It's just this idea I had. And this looks like a good spot for it." He gestured off to the side of the road.

Beyond the guardrail was a line of green bushes. I walked over and peered around the side and saw a beautiful grassy glen that was completely hidden from the road.

When I gave him a questioning look, he came over and grabbed me around the waist and lifted me into the air. "We're on the state line. And I thought maybe we could cross it . . . like, horizontally."

Horizontally? Was he saying what I thought he was saying?

"So we start in California and end up—" I began.

"In Nevada," he finished. He grinned. "You up for it?"

I started to laugh.

"Definitely." I told him. "Definitely."

Chapter 19

We'd better get going," I said, pulling on my helmet. "Looks like rain." The blue sky was giving way to nasty-looking gray clouds. "Besides, we've got something like forty-nine other state lines to christen. How far to Utah?"

Griffin smiled. "About ten minutes."

I was still laughing as we climbed back onto Griffin's bike. This is just the beginning, I thought as Griffin began to jump-start the bike.

The motor coughed. He tried again. This time there was a sort of wheezing sound. Then it died out.

"Aw, man!" He slid off the bike and bent down to check the engine.

"What's wrong?"

"Probably the coil. I thought it would last, but—man."

"Can you fix it?" I asked. Griffin is good with bikes.

He usually does all the work on his engine. Sometimes he spends all day tinkering with it.

"No. No, we'll have to get a tow into town." He rolled the bike toward the highway so that we could flag down a passing car.

I yanked off my helmet and followed, wondering how we could be so unlucky to break down at the beginning of spring break.

It's just a minor setback, I told myself. We'll get to a repair shop and get this puppy back on the road in no time.

Just then thunder boomed in the distance. Griffin and I turned to each other as the rain started to fall— a hard, soaking rain. He propped the bike up on its stand at the side of the road, reached into his pocket, and pulled out a harmonica.

A harmonica!

"Are you kidding me?" I demanded as he started playing a bluesy tune. "I feel like I'm in some fugitive movie."

And then we just laughed.

As it turned out, our "minor setback" became a major delay. The mechanic at the gas station in Nevada didn't know what the problem was. Besides, he didn't have parts, and he acted like it would take weeks to get them there.

"We've got to get back to San Francisco," Griffin told me. "There's a guy there that I always deal with. Carter. He'll be able to get the bike running again."

We rode back to San Francisco in the tow truck. Probably a ridiculously expensive ride, but I didn't want to know about it. I mean, Griffin had enough money to buy an entirely new bike for this trip. But I knew enough to avoid mentioning that. Guys have this attachment to their bikes and cars, and it's something you do not want to mess with.

Carter, the bike guru, turned out to be a guy in his forties who looked like he slept in his greasy coveralls.

"The guy in this little town in Nevada thought it was the condenser," Griffin told him as they both bent over the bike, checking valves and hoses.

"More likely your coil," Carter said.

"That's what I tried to tell him," Griffin said. "Either way, he didn't have the part."

"Right," I jumped in, trying to hurry things along. "We thought we could get it fixed faster here at home and then take off again—"

"Your condenser's fine," Carter told Griffin as if I weren't even in the garage. "So it's definitely the coil. You must have been running her on—"

"One cylinder," Griffin finished. "The electric's funky, but I thought I had the kinks worked out."

I frowned, put off by the bike-speak. They could go on about cylinders and coils all day. "Can you fix it?" I asked point-blank. "We already lost a day. And we're in a hurry, so . . ."

"What?" Carter scratched his head, as if he'd just heard the question for the first time. "Oh, sure. I got a couple of coils around here somewhere." He turned toward this big wall of shelves and started rooting through a grimy box. "Have to look, though. Everything's packed up."

"Packed up?" Griffin frowned. "What's—"

"Yeah." Carter nodded. "Selling the shop. But I got the coils somewhere. And you know what else? You ever thought about an electronic ignition?"

"Sweet." Griffin smiled like a kid on Christmas

morning. "And maybe a Bonneville head and some weber carbs—"

"Whoa, whoa, wait," I interrupted. "We don't need carbs. And we don't need . . . heads. What we need is—what, a coil, right? Just a coil." When Carter looked at me as if he didn't understand English, I added, "We're kind of in a hurry."

The mechanic shrugged. "Okay. Be done in the morning."

"Excellent," I said, fighting the urge to physically drag Griffin out of there.

He seemed dazed as he surveyed the mounds of boxes in the shop, then nodded. "Yeah, a coil," he said finally.

"Maybe it's lucky that we broke down," I told Griffin the next morning as he poked his head into my attic room. I held up my toothbrush. "I forgot to pack this the first time. Would've been brushing my teeth with twigs."

He nodded, his eyes flashing with excitement and something else . . . almost nervousness.

"Everything okay with the bike?" I asked.

"Yeah, yeah. And what you said about luck? You know, it's true. Because if we didn't break down, we wouldn't have ended up back here, at the shop. And—and I wouldn't have talked to Carter—"

"Who wouldn't have fixed your bike so we could hit the road again today," I said happily. "See? It's luck. Sort of our fate."

"Well . . ." he hesitated. "Sort of. See, the thing is, we can't take off."

"What do you mean, can't?" I started getting this

nervous feeling. Was spring break about to slip through my fingers?

"It's like you were saying, how one thing leads to the next for a reason. Like our trip being blown—"

"Well, it's not exactly *blown*," I pointed out.

"And now I've got this, like, totally amazing opportunity."

I shook my head blankly. "What? What opportunity?"

"I told Carter I'd buy it, Jule," he said excitedly. "The bike shop."

"What?" I squinted at him.

"I'm going to use my money to buy the shop."

I couldn't think of anything to say. I just stared at him.

How could he? I mean, it wasn't just that he was ruining spring break. He was digging in, settling down just like everyone else.

That wasn't the way it was supposed to be. Griffin was my ticket out of here. We were supposed to go off—together. Exploring. Testing our wings.

But now he was stuck in the mud.

Chapter 20

I couldn't stand it. The thought of Griffin sinking all his money—money that was supposed to buy us our freedom—into that smelly old dusty bike shop. . . . I just couldn't take it.

So I sat down in the kitchen with a list of business considerations and tried to show Griffin that he could still get out of the deal. That he *had* to get out of the deal.

"You made an oral agreement, subject to inspections and God knows what else," I told him. "It's totally nonbinding."

He ducked his head into the fridge and reappeared with a can of soda. "I don't want to get out of it."

"Yeah?" I looked down at the list. "What's Carter's average monthly net profit?"

"He says he brings in about three or four grand, easy."

"That's gross," I pointed out.

"What's so gross about it?" he joked. "It's good money."

"Griffin! You're buying a business here, not deodorant. Haven't you asked him anything?"

His shoulders sank and I could feel him getting all defensive. "Well, sure. I asked him how much business he gets. And he says he stays busy all the time, so—"

"There was nobody in there the other day," I pointed out. "We were the only customers in sight."

"It was two o'clock on a weekday. On Saturdays you can't get near the place. I've been there. I've seen it."

"Okay, okay," I said, checking my list. "But does he own or rent the building? Because if he rents, you need to know the terms of the lease. And—"

"I'm going to have Arnie check all that stuff out for me." He leaned back against the sink, a wary look in his eyes. "This is a good thing," he said. "You should be excited for me."

"I am," I insisted. But my voice lacked conviction.

"I can do this." He gave me a hard look. "You have to trust me."

"This isn't about you screwing up or me trying to tell you what to do," I told him, trying to keep my voice from shaking. "It's about us, and the things I thought we'd do together."

He just stared at me, not getting it.

Gazing down at the kitchen counter, I felt tears stinging my eyes. "There's this story in Greek mythology. This guy named Icarus, who wanted to fly. He got this amazing pair of man-made wings. And they worked. He flapped his wings and he could fly."

I looked at Griffin. He was following the story intently.

"But Icarus loved flying so much that he went too high. He got too close to the sun, and his wings melted." A tear slid down my cheek, and I quickly wiped it away. "That's how I feel now. You came home. The lawsuit . . . I mean, it's like someone gave us wings. We could have taken off—together. But it was too great. We got too close to the sun, and—" My voice broke as a knot formed in my throat. "And now our chances have all melted away."

He came up behind me and wrapped his arms around me. "It's not that way. Really," he whispered. "We'll still be together. This is a good thing."

I wanted to believe him. I really did.

But inside, I had this terrible feeling that he was wrong.

For a while I kept hoping that for some reason the bike shop deal would fall through. Maybe Arnie would uncover some problem, or Carter would change his mind about selling.

But for once, things sailed along smoothly. Before the school year was out, Griffin was the owner free and clear, and he spent most of his time in that grimy garage, tinkering and trying out things and talking bike talk. He was totally into it, which depressed me even more.

That left me with time to kill—lots of time. That's how I ran into Justin that day at the Coffee House. He had just heard that he'd gotten into Yale. He was totally up.

"Time to hit your parents up for a convertible," I teased him. I sat on the arm of the couch and picked up the book he'd been reading—a travel guide to Europe.

"I've already struck," he said. "They're giving me a plane ticket, a backpack, and enough cash for two months in Europe."

"The backpacking trip," I said, feeling a twinge of jealousy. That could have been me. Me and Griffin. "So . . . is Robyn going, too?"

"Can't," he answered, putting his coffee mug aside. "She's doing that archaeological thing through Berkeley. We thought we'd hook up for a few weeks in Greece."

"Greece." I nodded. "Sounds nice."

"So how about you? You heading off with Griffin?"

I shook my head. "He's, like, overwhelmed these days." I explained about the bike shop, adding, "He's doing okay, but it's pretty demanding."

"Which leaves you on your own, sort of," Justin said. Then he gave me a sideways look. "Hey. You want to hear a crazy idea? Actually, it's not so crazy. Not at all."

"What? What?" I pressed, smiling.

"Okay." Justin leaned forward. "What would Griffin think if you and I . . ."

"No way," Griffin said flatly. "No way are you going backpacking through Europe with Justin. I mean, why is he, like, out of the blue asking you to go away with him? Because you used to go out? Does he think that once he gets you away from me—"

"Come on!" I interrupted. "It's not about that. He has a girlfriend. Only she can't go."

"Right." He banged the door of the bike shop open, and we both walked out. The shop was in an ugly, noisy industrial area, which always reminded me of the zillion better ways that Griffin could have spent his money.

He went over to a pylon and kicked it. "I've been back a month, and you want to go away already."

"It's not about leaving you," I said. How could I explain it to him? That I felt trapped? That my life had hit a dead end? "I want to travel and get all kinds of weird jobs and stay in weird places and figure things out. You know that. I told you that on day one. And every day since."

He stared off, looking hurt.

"All I want is two months in Europe," I said to his silence.

His lips thinned. "With *him.*"

"With *you*," I protested. "But you've got stuff that's keeping you here. And you don't want to go . . . and he does."

"No way." When he looked up, his eyes were cold and his expression—it was as if I'd stabbed him in the back. "Do what you have to do, Julia. But remember this: If you to Europe with that guy, it's over."

"What?" I gasped. Was he kidding me?

"You heard me," he said. "If you go, it's over between you and me."

Chapter 21

I was steaming mad when I left the bike shop that day. I mean . . . an *ultimatum!* Griffin actually laid down the law, as if he could control me. That floored me. I could feel myself about to explode and go nuts and break up with him on the spot.

But something made me hold back. Take some time to sort this out, I thought. And before some devastating words slipped out of my mouth, I slipped out of there.

I swung by Sarah's house. She introduced me to a handful of ladies who were there to play bridge with her mother. "Well, I'd better go," she told them politely. "Julia and I have plans."

"We do?" I asked, mystified.

She flashed me a desperate look that said: Get me out of here! "We *do*," I said decisively.

We drove west to Ocean Beach, where the wind

makes the surf wild and rough so you don't have to put up with swimmers and sunbathers.

"Thanks for bailing me out," Sarah said. We sat with the car doors open as we pulled off our boots and socks. "Ten more minutes with the ladies and I was going to get grilled on how hearts beat spades, or something like that. Sometimes I think I should have opted to go to school back east." Sarah was planning to attend Berkeley in the fall.

"No problem," I said, tying my hair back. The sun was high in the clear sky, and the sand felt hot underfoot as we walked along. "I needed to get out. Blow off some steam."

"Well, it's a totally gorgeous day," Sarah said, raking back her brown hair. "So we're in the right place."

"Sure," I said. "Here we are on a beautiful beach. Sunshine and wind and crashing waves. Totally romantic. So what's wrong with the picture?"

Sarah laughed. "Don't tell me you need Griffin to have a good time? Come on, Jule. Can't you enjoy something without him by your side?"

I gritted my teeth. "This just wasn't the way I expected things to be after Griffin got back. We were supposed to be together. Testing our wings together."

"Instead, Griffin is alone, testing spark plugs. Right?"

"That's the least of it," I muttered. I told her about the backpacking trip with Justin. About how I was dying to go, and how Griffin threatened to break up with me if I did.

"Whoa! An ultimatum?" Her dark eyes grew wide. "I've never known you to put up with something like that. Why didn't you dump him on the spot?"

Now, that was a good question. Because the old Julia would have broken up with him right then and there.

"I don't know," I confessed. "Things just aren't as black and white as they used to be. I've begun to see gray areas."

I glanced up at Cliff House, the restaurant built up on the jagged rocks near the shoreline. "Did you ever see pictures of the old Cliff House?" I asked Sarah.

She cupped a hand over her eyes and squinted up at the cliff. "That big Victorian inn? It was like a giant fancy wedding cake perched on the rocks."

"Exactly. It always looked like it was ready to slide right into the ocean. And that's the way my life has been recently. Balanced on the edge. Tilting."

She nodded. "Yeah. It's been a tough year."

"But through all the chaos, Griffin was sort of like a lifeline. Even when he wasn't here, I kept reaching out to him, writing to him, thinking about him."

Sarah stopped walking to face me. "You love him a lot, huh?"

I nodded. "More and more all the time. He sort of . . . made me evolve. He made me less selfish."

"I've noticed." Sarah's eyes were warm, understanding. "You've changed, Jule."

"And Griffin has, too. He's growing up. Making a life." I kicked at the sand. "I mean, I totally despise that grimy bike shop. But I have to admit that it was a good thing for Griffin. He's found something that he wants to do, something he's passionate about. I have to be glad about that."

"Sounds like you have a lot to be glad about," Sarah said. "So . . . does this mean you're *not* going to Europe with Justin?"

I nodded. "It's going to kill me. But I'll give it up."

"Wow." Sarah whistled. "I wonder if Griffin will realize what a big deal this is. Are you going to tell him tonight?"

I sat down on a huge rock and buried my feet deep in the sand. "After the way he laid down the law?" I shook my head. "No way. I mean, I love him. But he has to learn not to treat me that way. No, I figure he can just twist in the wind a day or two."

"So—uh—so anyway . . ." I tried to explain things to Justin the next day in class. "I guess I'm not going."

"Hold on." Justin put his hands flat on his desk. "I'm not getting this. I mean, he *knows* I'm with Robyn, right?"

I nodded, feeling like an idiot.

"So why don't you just tell him he's got nothing to worry about and come get a Eurailpass with me?"

"I *can't*, Justin," I said. I turned and walked toward the classroom door.

Of course, he couldn't let it drop. "You *can't?*" He protested, following me out to the corridor. "You mean you're just going to let him kill the whole thing? What kind of relationship do you guys have if—"

"Griffin!" I said in surprise. There he was, leaning against a row of lockers. Waiting for me.

Justin stopped in his tracks. "I'm, uh . . . late for calc." He slung his backpack over his shoulder and disappeared.

"Hey," I said as the bell rang and the halls started to empty out.

"You were probably ragging on me just now, huh?" Griffin asked. When I frowned, he added, "It's okay. I'm mad at me, too. I don't like standing in the way of stuff for you, Julia. I want to say *go*. Go and see amazing things and come back and tell me all about them and I love you. I *want* to say that."

"So why can't you?" I asked. My voice was the only sound in the silent corridor.

"I'm trying to get there. I am." His eyes were so sincere, so full of love. "And I think there might be a way . . . a way to make this work."

My jaw dropped. "You do?"

He nodded toward the door, and we ducked out quickly, before any of the school administrators spotted us. "So . . ." I prodded as we crossed the parking lot to my car. "Are you going to tell me, or do I have to pry it out of you?"

"Not here," he said, yanking open the door. I tossed him the keys, and he slid behind the wheel and drove off.

We ended up in the Presidio, this park of rolling green hills overlooking the bay. Griffin found a bench with an incredible view, one of those spots where the water and the Golden Gate Bridge and the trees and buildings look beautiful and unreal, like a toy train village right at your fingertips. One of those places where you look out and think, yeah, anything is possible. Anything can happen.

"Listen," he said, weaving his fingers through mine. "I know I was harsh yesterday. That stuff I said to you—I don't think it came out exactly right."

I gave him a look. "No kidding."

"It's just that I don't . . . I don't trust things."

"You don't trust *me.*"

"No, I trust you," he insisted. "I don't trust, like, life."

I sighed. It sounded so lame.

"I've been running through this list in my head. This list of bad possibilities," he said. "Do you want to hear? You fall in love with Justin. Or . . . or you have a big fight with Justin, and you feel lonely and you fall in love with someone else. Some French guy or something. Or . . . you find a job you really want in the most beautiful city you've ever seen. Or . . . you go to Rome and decide to be a nun."

I smiled.

"Or maybe I do something stupid. Like I'm rushing home to get your call and this heavy vault drops on my head."

That made me laugh. "Griffin, that happens only in cartoons."

"No," he insisted. "That's the kind of stuff that happens to us. Because we're not lucky, Jule. We have to be careful. Weird things happen to us. That's why I'm afraid to let you go. I'm scared to take my eyes off you."

My throat swelled. I gave him a warm, tight embrace. God, he was wonderful.

He stared out over the San Francisco Bay. "I know how important this trip is to you. And I think there's a way . . . a way that I can let you go without driving myself nuts," he said.

He took a deep breath, then turned to look me in the eyes. "What if—what if we get married first?"

Chapter 22

I stared at Griffin. I felt sort of like the wind was knocked out of me.

Married?

Marriage was something for older people, for couples, for brides and grooms. I mean, the word itself is just so . . . *institutional.*

But then, there was Griffin with his smoky eyes, his dark hair, and a love so intense that it took my breath away.

"God, Griffin," I choked. "This is, like, huge."

He nodded. "Yeah. But it's the only way. I mean, as long as I know that we're married, that you're my *wife,* I feel okay letting you go. I mean, then I know that you'll be coming back. Back to me. It seemed like a wild idea at first. But then, the more I thought about it. I don't know. It felt good." He shrugged. "So . . . what do you think?" His mouth twitched nervously.

I stared into his eyes—and I could see it.

Yes. I could definitely see it. After all the choices and changes I'd made in the past year, all the scary decisions, this was the one thing that felt totally right.

This was what I'd needed all the time.

"I think it's crazy. And . . . and I want it," I said slowly. "I want to marry you."

He pulled me into his arms for a breathless kiss.

"So . . ." I said when we came up for air. "When do you want to do this?"

"I don't know." He paused, then checked his watch. "How about . . . like . . . now?"

My heart thudded. "Now? Today?"

He nodded.

I bit my lip. What about my family? I'd have to tell them.

Not now, a little voice inside whispered. *Charlie will freak. He'll try to stop you. Tell him later.*

When it's too late for him to do anything about it.

I took a deep breath. "I never did believe in long engagements."

Griffin gave me this incredible smile. Then he pulled me close for another kiss.

And I knew I was doing the right thing.

"Hey. What about that guy Icarus?" Griffin asked as we walked to the car. "Does he ever get his wings back? Does he get a chance to fly again?"

"I don't remember," I said. "But *we* will."

It probably sounds totally corny, but when Griffin and I walked into the room with the justice of the peace and turned to face each other, I started to cry. Good tears, which is probably a first for me. I was getting married! *Married!*

Standing there in the judge's chambers, I felt more alive than ever before. I never imagined it would be this way. Not that I dreamed of weddings, but most girls picture themselves in something white. Instead, we wore baggy jeans and leather jackets. And that was just perfect, somehow.

And you know how you always see tons of flowers and family and friends? Well, Griffin and I were alone. But we had each other. And isn't that what marriage is really about? In some ways, it's the most personal thing you could ever do.

"Marriage is an honorable estate," the judge said solemnly. "It is not to be entered into lightly or unadvisedly, but reverently, discreetly, and soberly."

Griffin gave me a slight smile, and I knew how he was feeling. He was just as high on this whole thing as I was. We were totally in synch.

When the judge started to hand Griffin a laminated card so that he could read his vows, Griffin waved it off. He knew them. He knew the vows!

He took my hand and slowly, carefully said the words. "I, Griffin, take you, Julia, to be my wedded wife . . ."

Then it was my turn.

"I, Julia, take you, Griffin, to be my wedded husband," I whispered. Tears burned my eyes. "To have and to hold, from this day forward, for better or worse, for richer or poorer, in sickness and in health, to love and to cherish, as long as we both shall live."

The judge leaned forward. "Please place the ring on—"

"Oh," Griffin winced. "We don't—I didn't—"

"We don't have a ring," I told the judge.

"Sorry," Griffin whispered to me. "I—"

"It's okay," I assured him.

"Well, then . . ." The judge cleared his throat. "Inasmuch as Griffin and Julia have consented together in marriage, by virtue of the authority vested in me, I pronounce you husband and wife."

And that was it . . . we were married.

Married.

The judge looked at us, waiting for something. I wasn't sure if we were supposed to kiss or give him a tip or let out a big hurray. But it was such an enormous moment, so huge, and I just wanted to savor it.

"I love you," Griffin whispered to me.

I felt as if bright flowers were blossoming inside me. "I love you, too."

We were together—really together, legally and everything. And it felt so good. So perfect. So many loose ends in my life had come together with Griffin.

Now there was just one more thing.

Breaking the news to my family.

Chapter 23

Griffin kicked his room door open and hoisted me into his arms.

I laughed, feeling giddy and wild. "What are you doing?"

"It's that threshold thing," he said, stumbling in through the doorway. He lurched toward the bed, spilling me onto it. I bounced onto the mattress, and he dove on beside me.

"Oh, hello," I teased, as if surprised to see him.

"Howdy," he said in a low, sexy voice. "Did we just—?"

"Umm-hmm. We sure did." Neither of us could believe it.

He ran his hand up my arm, sending delicious shivers through me. I closed my eyes for a moment, then sat up. "You know, I should call them," I said. "Let them know."

"Your family?" Griffin reached up and pulled me back and planted a long kiss on my lips.

"Tomorrow," he whispered. His hand slid from my neck down to my shoulder, then inside my jacket. "Call them tomorrow."

He pressed against me and we rolled across the bed. And I didn't need any more convincing.

"Julia?" Charlie called when I poked my head in through the kitchen door the next morning. "Is that you?"

I stepped in nervously. "I, uh . . . I didn't expect you to be home." In fact, I'd been hoping that maybe I could start out by breaking the news to someone easy. Like Owen.

But there they all were. Charlie, Bailey, Claudia, and Owen. All of my siblings, rushing through the morning with the usual Salinger sense of chaos.

"Listen, Jule," Charlie started in. "Not to be too much of a parent or anything, but where have you been the last twenty-four hours?"

"Hey, Griffin," Claudia called as he walked in behind me.

"Well," Bailey said, "guess that answers that."

They went back to packing lunches and figuring out who was carpooling with whom. I looked back at Griffin, and he nodded.

Now was as good a time as any. I took a deep breath.

"Griffin and I went to a justice of the peace yesterday," I announced. "We got married."

Silence. Everyone stopped in their tracks.

"Because . . . because we love each other," I said, finding it difficult to go on. Suddenly my confidence was evaporating, especially when it came time to face Charlie. "We're old enough," I went on. "And we want to be together. Forever."

Taking in their blank faces, I added, "And—and you'll get used to it," before I turned and walked out of the kitchen.

My chest felt tight as I paused at the bottom of the stairs. This was even harder than I'd thought it would be.

What were they all thinking? Did they hate me? Did they think I was abandoning them?

Griffin came up behind me and touched my shoulder. "Is it me, or was that like a walk through the North Pole?"

I nodded. "You'd better go . . . take care of that stuff at the shop," I told him, trying to pull myself together. "I'll pack my stuff. You can swing by and pick me up when you're done."

"You okay?" he whispered. When I nodded, he gently kissed me on the lips and squeezed my hand. "Don't let 'em get you down. Because this is going to be great. Really."

I forced a smile, then watched as he let himself out the front door. I half expected Claudia or Bailey to come out of the kitchen. To ask me questions. At least to say "congratulations."

But no one appeared. God, that hurt.

My heart was beating fast as I ran upstairs. I got out a suitcase and started emptying the drawers from my dresser. I felt sort of panicked, like I had to escape, get away before they stopped me.

No! I thought.

I took a deep breath and sank onto the bed. No, I wasn't running away. I was moving onto a new life, and there was no rush. Because this was the right thing to do. I'd made the right choice, and I didn't have to be ashamed of it.

"Hey." I glanced up. Charlie stood in the doorway. "Can we talk about this?"

"There isn't a lot to say, Charlie," I said warily. "I love him. He loves me."

"Okay, so be in love. No one's saying you shouldn't. Spend every second of every day together if you want. But, God, Jule, *this*. This is so . . ."

"It's huge, I know," I admitted. "It kind of takes my breath away, too."

"It should. I mean, to run off and get *married*. Have you even thought about what that means?"

My jaw clenched in anger. There he went again. Treating me like a child. "Of course," I said flatly.

"For how long? A minute? An hour? Did you think about it for twenty-four hours?"

"I thought about it when he asked me," I snapped, turning away from him to collect the stuff in the vanity. God, why couldn't Charlie just back off and be happy for me?

I didn't want to fight. I wouldn't. If I'd learned anything from our earlier war, it was that I couldn't just snarl back every time Charlie tried to play the parent.

With a deep breath, I turned back to my oldest brother. "You know, Charlie, when I said yes, it felt like the rightest thing I've ever done in my life. With that one word, everything just snapped into place. It's like—Griffin loves me and we're going to be together forever, which means I can go anywhere, do anything, and I'll have that. I'll have him. And I love *him,* so he can stop worrying he's going to lose me and just relax and become this—this man he needs to be."

He shook his head. But he didn't say anything.

"I know you think I've made a mistake," I told him.

"Yes."

"So let me make it."

"You're my little sister," Charlie said protectively.

"But I'm not a little girl anymore. Everything changes, Charlie. Look at me. I'm all grown-up. And I need to live my own life."

Charlie did look at me then, and I read something different in his eyes. It wasn't a repeat of the tired old argument we always seemed to have. He seemed to be studying me, trying to understand. At least he was *trying*.

But I still don't think he got it. With a final shake of his head, he left the room. I went back to my packing with an empty feeling in the pit of my stomach.

Dragging my suitcase down the attic stairs, I felt excited . . . and sad, too. I mean, this thing with Griffin was like taking off in a rocket. We really were going flying together.

I just wished my family could appreciate the ride.

Claudia and Bailey were waiting for me when I lugged my suitcase into the front hall.

"Griffin picking you up?" Bailey asked.

"Yeah. He's going to honk," I said. Suddenly I felt really uncomfortable in my own house. "Maybe I'll wait outside."

"No! Wait!" Claudia protested. "You can't leave like this. I mean, this is supposed to be a really important day. A really wonderful day."

"Yeah, well, nobody feels like celebrating with me," I said. I glanced over at Charlie, who stood back in the shadows. Not part of the farewell committee.

"It's hard, Jule," Bailey complained. "Come on. This is a lot to drop on us. Maybe with a few months' notice and a big ceremony . . ."

I shook my head. "That was never going to happen, Bay."

"We . . . uh, got something for you. From all of us," Claudia said. She pulled a small velvet box out of her pocket.

"Are you kidding?" My breath caught in my throat. It was a total surprise.

Carefully, I took the box and popped it open. A thin gold band winked back at me.

"Mom's wedding ring," said Claudia.

My throat suddenly felt so tight, I couldn't even answer. It was such a special gift. And I didn't have a ring. It was sort of like fate . . . the chance that I'd been taking all along.

"You're the first one of us, Jule," Bailey said softly.

"Try it on," Claudia said.

As I fumbled with the box, I asked, "This is *really* from all of you?"

Claudia nodded, but I needed to hear it from him. "Charlie?"

He hesitated. At last, he said, "I want you to be happy, Julia. I really do."

It wasn't exactly a blessing. But at least he was meeting me halfway. I smiled through my tears at my big brother.

"Go ahead," he said. "Put it on."

I slipped the gold band on my finger and stared at it.

"Look at it," I said, choked with emotion. "It sparkles."

Everyone leaned forward to see the ring on my finger as the horn sounded outside. Time to go.

With a tear-streaked smile, I hoisted the suitcase and took one last, long look at my family. It may sound corny, but I'll never forgot what I saw in their eyes.

Love.

Then I opened the door and headed out to Griffin's car to begin my new life.

The life that I had chosen.

party of five™

Join the party!

Read these new books based on the hit TV series.

#1 Bailey:
On My Own

#2 Julia:
Everything Changes

POCKET
B O O K S

Available
From Archway Paperbacks
Published by Pocket Books

© 1997 Columbia Pictures Television, Inc. All Rights Reserved. 1425-01

You Could Win A Party Of Five Party In Your Own Home!

party of five™

1 GRAND PRIZE

A "party of five" Party which will include a wide-screen TV, party provisions for the night to include pizza, ice cream and soda and "party of five" T-shirts for the winner and ten friends

5 FIRST PRIZES
"party of five" sweatshirt

15 SECOND PRIZES
"party of five" baseball hat

25 THIRD PRIZES
"party of five" T-shirt

50 FOURTH PRIZES
"party of five" mug

COLUMBIA PICTURES TELEVISION
a SONY PICTURES ENTERTAINMENT company

Complete the entry form and mail to:
Pocket Books/"party of five" Sweepstakes
Advertising and Promotion Department
1230 Avenue of the Americas
New York, NY 10020

Name_____Birthdate___ /___/_____

Address_____

City_____State_____Zip_____

Phone (_____) _____

(See next page for official rules)

Pocket Books/"party of five" Sweepstakes Official Rules:

1. No Purchase Necessary. Enter by mailing the completed Official Entry Form (no copies allowed) or by mailing on a 3" x 5" card with your name and address, daytime telephone number and birthdate to the Pocket Books/"party of five" Sweepstakes, Advertising and Promotion Department, 13th Floor, 1230 Avenue of the Americas, NY, NY 10020. Sweepstakes begins 10/7/97. Entries must be received by 3/30/98. Not responsible for lost, late, damaged, stolen, illegible, mutilated, incomplete, or misdirected or not delivered entries or mail or for typographical errors in the entry form or rules. Entries are void if they are in whole or in part illegible, incomplete or damaged. Enter as often as you wish, but each entry must be mailed separately. Winners will be selected at random from all eligible entries received in a drawing to be held on or about 4/1/98. Winners will be notified by mail.

2. Prizes: One Grand Prize: A "party of five" party which will include a wide screen TV delivered to the winner's home a few days before the 1997-98 season finale, party provisions for the evening for the winner and ten friends, which will include pizza, ice-cream and soda and "party of five" T-shirts for the winner and ten friends *(approx. retail value $2,000.00)*, Five First Prizes: "party of five" sweatshirts *(approx. retail value $30 each)* Fifteen Second Prizes: "party of five" baseball caps *(approx. retail value $16.00 each)* , Twenty-five Third Prizes: "party of five" T-shirts *(approx. retail value $15.00 each)*. Fifty Fourth Prizes: "party of five" mugs *(approx. retail value: $7.50 each)*. The Grand Prize must be taken on the dates specified by sponsors.

3. The sweepstakes is open to legal residents of the U.S. and Canada (excluding Quebec) no older than fourteen as of 3/30/98, except as set forth below. Proof of age is required to claim prize. Prizes will be awarded to the winner's parent or legal guardian. Void in Puerto Rico and wherever prohibited or restricted by law. All federal, state and local laws apply. Sony Pictures Entertainment Inc., Columbia Pictures Television, Inc., Simon & Schuster, Inc., Parachute Properties and Parachute Press, Inc. (individually and collectively "Parachute"), their respective officers, directors, shareholders, employees, suppliers, parents, subsidiaries, affiliates, agencies, sponsors, participating retailers, and persons connected with the use, marketing or conduct of this sweepstakes are not eligible. And family members living in the same household as any of the individuals referred to in the immediately forgoing sentence are not eligible.

4. One prize per person or household. Prizes are not transferable and may not be substituted except by sponsors, in the event of prize unavailability, in which case a prize of equal or greater value will be awarded. All prizes will be awarded. The odds of winning a prize depend upon the number of eligible entries received.

5. If a winner is a Canadian resident, then he/she must correctly answer a skill-based question administered by mail.

6. All expenses on receipt and use of prize including federal, state and local taxes are the sole responsibility of the winners. Winners will be notified by mail. Winners may be required to execute and return an Affidavit of Eligibility and Release and all other legal documents which the sweepstakes sponsor may require (including a W-9 tax form) within 15 days of attempted notification or an alternate winner may be selected.

7. Winners or winners' parents on winners' behalf agree to allow use of their names, photographs, likenesses, and entries for any advertising, promotion and publicity purposes without further compensation to or permission from the entrants, except where prohibited by law.

8. Winners agree that Sony Pictures Entertainment Inc., Columbia Pictures Television, Inc., Simon & Schuster, Inc., Parachute, and their respective officers, directors, shareholders, employees, suppliers, parents, subsidiaries, affiliates, agencies, sponsors, participating retailers, and persons connected with the use, marketing or conduct of this sweepstakes, shall have no responsibility or liability for injuries, losses or damages of any kind in connection with the collection, acceptance or use of the prizes awarded herein, or from participation in this promotion. By participating in this sweepstakes, participants agree to release, discharge and hold harmless Sony Pictures Entertainment Inc., Columbia Pictures Television, Inc., Simon & Schuster, Inc., Parachute, and their respective officers, directors, shareholders, employees, suppliers, parents, subsidiaries, affiliates, agencies, sponsors, participating retailers, and persons connected with the use, marketing or conduct of this sweepstakes from any injuries, losses or damages of any kind arising out of the acceptance, use, misuse or possession of any prize received in this sweepstakes.

9. By participating in this sweepstakes, entrants agree to be bound by these rules and the decisions of the judges and sweepstakes sponsors, which are final in all matters relating to the sweepstakes.

10. For a list of major prize winners, (available after 4/5/98) send a stamped, self-addressed envelope to Prize Winners, Pocket Books/"party of five" Sweepstakes, Advertising and Promotion Department, 13th Floor, 1230 Avenue of the Americas, NY, NY 10020. "party of five" and the "party of five" logo are trademarks of Columbia Pictures Television, Inc. No celebrity endorsement implied. © 1997 Columbia Pictures Television, Inc. All rights reserved.